MOTORBONT

THE NOVELIZATION

BRIAN G. BERRY

BASED ON THE ORIGINAL SCREENPLAY BY
MARK POLONIA

ENCYCLOPOCALYPSE
PUBLICATIONS

Encyclopocalypse Publications
www.encyclopocalypse.com

Vintage Mass Market Edition
ISBN: 978-1-960721-49-5

Cover Layout by Sean Duregger
Cover Artwork Elements Used by Permission by SRS Cinema, LLC
Interior design and formatting by Sean Duregger
Edited by Danielle Yeager, Hack & Slash Editing

FOREWORD

BY MARK POLONIA

As far back as I can remember, the very first novelization of a movie I had ever held in my grubby, pre-pubescent hands was STAR WARS. I had already seen the film, and was eager to relive the experience through the gold bordered book with the films poster on the cover. As I read it fervently, I realized there was more to the book that I saw on screen, or at least remembered. I got into the heads of the characters, their motivations, fears and dreams. It was quite a gob smack for someone who saw it as surface level popcorn entertainment.

Many years later, I bought THE BLACK HOLE novelization, and again, it was a different experience than the film, owing in parts to the fact that novelizations are often written based on original shooting scripts and don't reflect what ultimately ends up on screen. Look no further than the KING KONG novel from the 1933 classic. It contains paragraphs of Kong on Dinosaur violence we can only wish they had the budget to realize.

Here we are now........decades later, and novelizations are still at the core of film literature. Never, and I mean NEVER in my wildest imagination, would I have ever guessed that one of my micro-budget efforts have taken the same literary course, but here we are. The nice thing about writing is you aren't wrestling with budgets, weather, locations falling through, effects failing and actor unavailability. It's just pure writing, the author and the word. An envious position for anyone who has attempted to take words on paper, from a script, and dare to make it come alive. The pen is mightier than the sword, but in reality, it is mightier than the lens.

Enjoy the writing before you in this wonderful novel.....it can take you places our budget wouldn't let us go!

Mark Polonia
2024

SRS

PRESENTS

MOTORBOAT

PROLOGUE

Candles flickered around the room, burning holes in the dark. A soothsayer cloaked in an aspect of woolen shadow drew power and wisdom from the crystal orb her black nails prowled. Voices drifted, their authors inhibited into bleak and hazy profiles in the compressing dark.

"Tell me what you see …" Father Thomas asked her, anticipation rising in his voice.

Silence held its grip before her voice, a hissing sibilance more in line with a bag of serpents, spoke. "What you ask for is in a dark place—"

"I want to know—"

"*Silence!* I need to concentrate to send my soul to see in such a terrible place."

"If you find it, I can stop it … here and now."

Dismissing the eye of the cloudy orb, the soothsayer directed her energies over the forbidden Black Tome opened in front of her. On its yellowed parchment pages were illustrated strange symbols and alchemies of ancient wisdom; crude and malignant designs. It was from this that her wisdom into the dark realms was consolidated and drawn from.

"Evil, that has existed for so long cannot be vanquished so easily, even by someone with so much faith …"

In a world admitted only to her eyes, a vast and nebulous horror emerges, bringing with it lurking shapes and ghoulish visages, dripping teeth, and eyes of lambent crimson. The disconnected vapors of rotting corpses brought beneath the heel and dagger of black demons. An ocean of blood thrashed in the throes of a red storm; its waves crashing upon the innocent and drinking away their existence with a vampiric lust.

"I see … I see shadowy figures, full of hate and rage. I see twisted souls with no way of escape. I see … blood and carnage!"

"Where are they?!" Demanded Father Thomas, his fist a white ball of iron at his side. "What location is home to this evil cancer?!"

A well of undetermined leagues yawned before her eyes into some abysmal shadow-crawling crater, etched beyond the gentle black waves of a great lake.

"A deep, black pool of water … a dwelling nearby … it is all I can see. I cannot pass any farther, and you —you must not interfere by yourself!"

"*I must!*" he raged. "It needs to end now!"

A wicked grin curled her sleek, cruel, red lips. "Nothing ever ends … it takes on a different path. Beware … and be strong."

Father Thomas felt the shadows absorbing him as he stepped away from the cruel gleam of the soothsayer. She directed her eyes onto his and a laugh broke from her lips. A burst of terrible laughter with all the evil of her mystical travel into madness rushed up her throat. It was the high cackling of a witch over a boiling cauldron of child meat.

No man, however, beneath the shield of a benevolent Lord could stand the frequency of that damnable cachinnation. He tore away from her eyes and ran—ran from that shadow-haunting lair that was the pit of ethereal voices and secret monotones and furtive whispers.

Though he gleaned little of her wisdom in the dark fountain in which she drew, there was enough available to point him in the right direction.

By God's will, he would put an end to this terrible Brotherhood of Darkness.

1

Rocky was gathering the last of his fishing gear from the boat and humping it over to his car that sat in the parking lot only ten meters from the docks. It was such a good night. Not much of a haul, but that meant little when you were enjoying your time on the lake. That's all that really mattered—to him anyway.

This was his third night out in a row, and he was already planning a fourth. If his wife allowed him the time, that is. Julia, she could get quite controlling at times, but he never let it backfire on him. He would tell her what she wanted to hear and leave her satisfied. But while she would gloat in her victory, Rocky would be sketching out his next plot, his next fishing route.

Tomorrow, he was thinking of hitting Lodgers Point. He knew that Chief Barney Rayl wouldn't like that much. And whenever the older Chief caught wind of folks snatching trout in those waters, he'd come unglued and threaten to fine them double for their infractions. To Rocky, and most in the area, it was prime territory. It seemed the fish even knew it was a violation to hit those waters, too, and that's why there was always such an abundance of spawning and living over there.

Instead of taking his boat in there, he would often inflate a raft, his dark green one, and paddle out and stay near the banks, over where the reeds got thick. It helped him swing his line into spots where the lack of a proper shore inhibited a perfect cast. Some folks, like Ned and Orville, hit the Point regularly in their paddle boat, not giving a shit if Chief Rayl caught them in the act. They had so many fines stacked up that it didn't really matter anyway.

Stowing his gear in the bed of the pickup, he swung the lid on the cooler back and counted his catch.

Four trout tonight. With plenty of meat on their bones they should make a fine dinner, come tomorrow.

Closing the lid with his foot, he picked up the cooler and set it back into his pickup. It was such a sweet night. The stars were plenty and the moon was fat and full. It was much too nice to hop in his rig and go home. Leaning back into his truck, he popped a match off his thumb and set fire to a cigarette. He took some drags, enjoying the smell of the pine in the air. That's the thing about Lake Jude, pine was a redolent flavor in the air. It made you think of the high alpine country, but Lake Jude wasn't too high on the elevation scale. It was mostly flatland, all but the ridges on the eastern side of the lake. But one thing about the area, it wasn't lacking in trees and thick forest. It spread its roots out for thousands of acres in all directions. The lake itself was mostly an isolated place that saw many visitors and campers come striper season, which actually started up in a few weeks. Rocky was well prepared to spend his time catching striper; there was nothing like hooking some fresh striper and throwing them on the spit with a squirt of lemon and garlic. He could almost taste it.

Dragging off his smoke, he heard some rustling nearby, coming from a dark thicket across the parking lot. That was another thing about tonight—it was damn dark out there. Solid and bold, all contours of tree life lost their molding and became, essentially, murky black walls inhabited with shifting shadows and lunar spears. The wind was blowing across the lake, and from his spot he could see the silver ripples flinging over its surface.

Pulling the ember to the filter, he went to toss his cigarette when the sound of footsteps running up behind him took him by surprise. He turned, wide-eyed, expecting not what, but seeing the shape of a man in dark cloth from head to boot coming at him with a dagger raised in his hand. Rocky turned to face the lake and started to run. But the moment he did just that, two others of similar appearance were waiting for him.

Call it a catacomb, call it a grotto, call it a cave, whatever name you choose to label, it smelled all the same. It had an odious, awful effluvium of an atmosphere that started stinging his eyes right away. It made his guts crawl up into a slimy ball and threaten to vacate between his legs. He wanted to cough, but he couldn't. His mouth had been sealed over with enough duct tape to hold a cement pylon intact. He tried moving around, but that wasn't happening either. He was locked in heavy chains, both his wrists and his ankles. He could see candles around him; many candles guttering, possibly hundreds, ringing the room. But beyond that, there was nothing else to see, just blackness and the ever-pressing shadowy interior.

He heard the shuffling of feet nearby and the sounds of what could be whispers in the air. There was a strangeness to them though, they sounded distant, far off yet so near. It perplexed his senses. Gave him a chill.

Somebody was coming up behind him now, and his instincts were screaming at him to turn around and see who it could be, but that was impossible. Bound to that table as he was, there was no mobility of any kind. He felt like a fly stuck to a glue strip. Out of the corner of his eyes, he saw one of those dark shapes that ran out of the woods earlier and grabbed him. He vividly remembered the one with the dagger lifted above their head, then turning to run, but that was all he could recall. His head hurt, so he figured that whatever happened, they had given him a good clubbing to the skull with something hard.

Now another one of those dark shapes approached, this one on the left. Their faces were pockets of shadows beneath the hoods, their fingers were steepled. They were the whisperers. Another now, this one coming around to stand near his feet. Three of them in total.

Rocky felt sick. To say he had a bad feeling was too easy a way to describe it. His heart responded by speeding up a few beats. He said something, but even wasn't even sure what. If anything, he was screaming for help but it was muffled deeply by the tape.

As if to amplify the terror of the situation, there was a rush of cold wind blowing in from behind him. It was an icy gust that pained his bones. He was shaking, his body responding to this windy invader. A smell hit him right away. An awful, detestable odor that made him think of slaughterhouses in the high summer. Above him, a figure leaned over him, a mask on their face, but their body … nothing was right about it. It seemed to be a fusion of black smoke and electric flashes of iridescent purples and wavering, shadowy tendrils.

A blade shimmered like white fire in its hand before plunging deeply into Rocky's breast. Rocky's eyes rounded in his sockets, exploding with the pain. Beneath the layers of tape, blood seeped thickly at the seams, his agony was a muted struggle. Now the other three withdrew their own implements, these, finely honed hatchets of silver. In a quick flash, the edge of one hacked away his arm in a red spray of blood. Another crashed down onto his knee, cleaving through to the table below. Blood strung out in a thick channel that flung from the cavity. Another silver edge buried itself in his throat to the oak, ripping his head from his shoulders in a blast of blood.

They continued their morbid surgery beneath the eyes of their Master, who stood as a shadow stands, malevolent eyes of prismatic fire alight at the blood winging from their sacrifice.

2

Out there at the edge of the narrow dock that stretched into the gentle chop of the Lake Jude, Father Thomas stood as one stands when in great contemplation over matters that would shake the very world. A wind brushed down the slopes and through the forest that ringed the waters as he gazed out across its dark blue surface. In the distance, he could see the backbone of a heavily forested rise and cluttered at its foot the frames of homes with private access to the shore. It was a bucolic place at first glance, but to those with knowledge, it was a veritable bed of evil on the rise.

Parting the long gray coat that whipped about his shins in the breeze, he reached into the pockets of his black slacks and both hands filled out with two Glock 9mm pistols, chambered, and deadly. He felt the weight of these in his hands, the roughness of their grips against his palms, the metal texture of their frame. It had to be done, he knew, for if he let the evil fester much longer, the rot would spread its roots into the community. A calamity he could not allow. By the Glory of God and His Good Will and His mighty kingdom, he would spade this horror from the soil before it had a chance to flourish.

Concealing the pistols beneath his coat, he pulled on a pair of black gloves smug to the wrist and rolled down a black mask in which only the blue points of his eyes could be seen through the narrow, oval gap in the mask. Turning from the lake, he walked down the dock where his boat was moored. Freeing the rope, he set himself behind the wheel, grabbed the throttle, and thrust his hand forward. The small craft roved forward and left a spreading trail of dissipating foam behind its path.

Belts of lightning slashed across the belly of the dark sky, as rain drove in heavy sideways sheets, pelting the roof of the building. On the outside, it might have looked like some old place needing a touch-up, some fresh trim, and a bit of yard work; but on the inside, it was something else entirely. It was a place of *worship*. Not to the heavenly Father that sits high up on His cosmic throne, but of a sinister, repulsive, nameless God. A God to the ghouls and serpents, to the bone collectors and carrion eaters.

A babble of incoherency filled the murky cellar, a disjointed melody of wicked intonations and cackles drifted around the three robed figures emerging from the stone portal which led deeper into their sanctuary. All of them were a duplication of the last. Dark, brownish robes of heavy cloth obscured their bodies with a narrow rope of white at their hips. Ceremonial masks that depicted the visage of grim skulls covered their faces. They walked on through the narrow confines in sullen silence, their hands steepled beneath their chins.

Directed by the voices that guided their advance, they came into another room, this one large and low-ceilinged and flamed to light with a hundred wicks, and swollen shadows at the walls, so that all seemed to expand around them in endless profusion. They spread abreast of one another, awaiting the arrival of their Master. Heaped before their eyes on the surface of an oak table were the ragged, skeletal remains of a recent sacrifice; the tissues and muscles shaved away from the bones, sitting in dripping, blood seeping mounds.

Strung throughout the room were the hideous relics of the dead and conjure-man. Skulls leered with eyes of polished glass and gems. Blood sat in fire-reflecting puddles on the floor. The scent of death overpowered all other senses and even stung the sight.

Messiah Ward entered behind his flock into the grim cellar, appearing to drift on a bed of shadowy tendrils below. Adorning his face was an ancient fetish mask engraved with an evil, ebony grin of fangs and ritualistic etchings. Flaring around him in billowing ruffles were the silky wings of a black cloak that lay open down the center of his breast, revealing a lucent crimson top with a frilly white collar. Into the room of corpse-mist and Satanic whisperings delivered by the talons of the goat-headed apparition lurking in the corner, Messiah Ward took his post behind a podium flanked with guttering candles.

He addressed his acolytes in a voice that had in its resonation a deep and disturbing annexation of a demon's dominance. "My children, my flock, welcome. We have been gathered here for our final sacrifice as our Master calls us to a darker place, our shaman has seen it in a vision. We have been prosecuted through the ages for our service to our Lord, burned at the stake by infidels! Now, the time has arrived, for our fiery transition ... do not fear ... do not fear, the Brotherhood of Darkness shall reign!"

Messiah Ward reached his right hand out and took the dagger that lay on a sheet of red velvet. Its silver finish caught the candlelight as he brought the blade within inches of his face. The acolytes waited patiently for the rending to come. Messiah Ward ran its edge through the tissues of his wrist, then filled a chalice with the gushing reward.

He held it aloft for all to see. "Drink the life-giving fluid, as the hour draws near!"

He approached his congregation and offered the first man a drink. The servant grasped the chalice without hesitation and brought its rim to his lips and drank down the warm crimson. Finished, he passed on the chalice to the next man and the next, until their throats were lathered red with the Messiah's blood.

Messiah Ward stretched out his arms in supplication to his Lord as the acolytes quaffed the chalice dry. "We welcome your cold embrace, oh Master!"

Father Thomas came into the room with all the confidence of his God behind his actions. Both pistols thrust out menacingly, he stood there as the three cloaked men turned to face him: snarls beneath their masks, their eyes filmy and distant, changing, hands up and fingers hooked into claws.

"We've been expecting you ... old friend!" Messiah Ward cackled as he lowered his arms.

Pleasantries and speeches were for those who had doubts as to their purpose and intent. But there was no such doubt with Father Thomas. The room was suddenly a flashing maelstrom as the guns came alive and bullets tore out meaty holes in the nearest servant before he could so much as scream in death, dropping him to the floor in a crumpled bleeding tangle. A stream of metal ripped a jagged line in the next man's belly up to his face. He came apart in a gooey slop before collapsing. The third man dashed for the Father but was stitched across the throat, ropes of blood pissing from his neck as he fell with a choking scream to join the others.

Acrid powder smoke drifting around him, his ears ringing, Father Thomas swung the guns on the Messiah. The priest's eyes burned holes into the nemesis across from him. In this visual contest, they shared a mutual hatred of one another. Messiah Ward felt the energy of his Master running through his blood now. The time was near. No matter his bodily fate the gears had been set into motion. There was no stopping what was coming—even in death.

"Do what you came here to do!" the Messiah laughed.

Father Thomas' shouts of anger were lost in the cracking of gunfire raging from his fists. While most of his aim was errant, the final bullet of one gun crashed into the Messiah's face. His brains were sucked out the back of his skull to splatter on the altar behind him.

Father Thomas watched as the Messiah stood in place before staggering back and toppling over. Before stepping over to ensure the man was dead, he reloaded both pistols. As he walked on, shell casings scattered at his approach, and his eyes never left the bloody wreck below. Each of them was dead, he knew, but he still approached like maybe there was a spark of life left inside of each of them.

Coming to a stop at the body of the Messiah, he stared down at the meat of his face. Snaking fingers of smoke rose from the busted skull as a hand reached up and sank its fingers into Thomas' knee, a chilling cackle ripping from the gore of its face as blood sprayed from the pulpy rupture of the Messiah's death mask.

Father Thomas screamed as he fired both pistols

below. Bullets ate out great red holes in the body as the hand slowly released its grip and sank to the floor to lie still.

Breathing hard, smoke floating around him, the floor a wet carpet of blood, the air began to thin as he swallowed hard, thinking what he had seen could not be possible but knowing it was. Fearing that the others would harass him even in death, he approached each and emptied his ammo until all the bodies were smoking broken forms.

Pocketing the pistols, he left the cellar behind and headed to his boat.

Surprisingly, the storm had abated and now all was gray and wet, the air damp. At his boat now, he took the bundle of tarps he brought with him and tossed the heavy linen sacks over his shoulder as he walked back into the house. Back down in that murky den of death, he started to roll the bodies into grim, bleeding packages.

There was still one last thing to do before this all would be over.

With the bodies secured in his boat, Father Thomas cut across the choppy lake, its dark water parting as he drove on until he came to the center of the great lake. Killing the engine, he stood there a moment beneath the eye of the moon, staring at the four tightly wrapped rolls stacked in his boat that were flecked darkly with patches of blood.

Okay, he thought. *It's time to get this over with. It's time to do what I set out to do.*

With some effort, he grabbed up the first body and forced it over the gunwale into the water. It gave a splash before it started to fade as it sank out of sight.

"Relish in your final journey to the dark abyss!" he told the sinking corpse.

He continued to offload each corpse until the boat rocked with their removal. He stared down into the inky surface, reddened by blood, watching as the bubbling water closed over the last one.

You've done well. The Lord will reward you for what you have done. You have no reason to feel guilt about what you have accomplished here. Their death was the vanquishing of evil. Rejoice in your service!

Convincing himself of the righteousness of his work, he sat down heavily, put the throttle in gear, and took off into the starry night.

3
_____

Two Years Later

It was the perfect time to do a bit of night fishing.

Or so they thought.

They made it to their spot just before the west ate up the remaining sunlight. Now, with everything around them bluing and hazing with the onset of the moon's dominance, they sat in their small paddle boat at the edge of some bushy reeds and ducktails, their lines out in the water, waiting. They were hoping to catch some of the trout around them in abundance, nipping at the gnats and mosquitoes and flies out there on the surface, but so far, they hadn't gotten a single bite, not a nibble.

It made sense if they thought about it for any amount of time. Why would the fish worry about worms on a hook when they had easy pickings on the surface? They would have been better off with a fly rod on the shore and a six-pack in a cooler. As it was, the boat was too small to have a cooler brought along with them as their knees were only a few inches apart from touching. But they had waited all day for the hours to pass at work to get some time at their favorite spot in the paddle boat.

Ned, a man of about fifty, with long red hair, more of it on his face, dressed in a jean jacket and pants, kept stealing glances at his friend, Orville. Something was off about him tonight. He had a funny look in his eye like he was scoping out for something that didn't want to show itself to him. It was the water that had his attention more than almost anything else, even fishing. Any other time, Ned wouldn't have minded. But that look there in his eye was starting to get the hairs standing on his neck.

Now, keep in mind, Orville was a big man, muscular and strong, with short dark hair flecked with some gray, a thick beard and mustache, and dark brows. He was dressed in a black long-sleeve shirt and olive-green pants. So why the man should be worried about anything—especially on this lake— troubled Ned.

"What is it?" he finally asked.

Orville looked at his friend like he didn't hear him the first time. Maybe his mind was elsewhere, particularly on the mirror black surface of the lake and the reeds on the bank and the dark trees and the shadows hanging in between.

"Huh?"

Ned tried to lighten the situation up a pinch by waving the air between his crotch. "Was it my beans … from earlier? You look … *distressed*."

Orville glanced around, seeming to look beyond where they were right then and into things he couldn't rightly see with a sane pair of eyes. He sniffed around like some hound that had lost its trail. "The air, it's so still, *funny-like*."

Ned laughed, reeling his line in before checking

that the bait was still kicking and swinging it back out there. "You sound like a scared child."

But Orville shook his head, staring off into the woods out there in front of him, his focus on the brooding shadows, then sweeping the shore, and finally back to the lake. "Nothing's been the same around here, since ..."

Ned was waiting for him to finish, but Orville sort of lost his voice and just kept staring, peeking around at things, listening to things that only he could hear. A night wind pushed into them, sending a ripple of water to edge up their boat.

In a sarcastic voice, he said, "Since ... *what?* The suspense is killing me."

Orville came alive, shaking the boat as his voice grew loud and all that was on his mind came pouring right out unabashed in a volcanic shout. *"The massacre of Messiah Ward and his followers!"*

Ned smiled as he cast his line out again, and watched as the red and white bobber sailed into the night before splashing thirty feet away. "That creep and his flock deserved what they got. Probably a secret op moved in on him. It was about time." He laughed in mockery before spitting over the boat. "The Brotherhood of Darkness brought no good to anyone."

Still convinced something wasn't right as the night became thicker and the sounds of limbs cracking out in the woods and their boughs being shaken by the wind were becoming a strain on his head, not to mention the patter of things unseen out in the water around them, maybe even *under* their boat right now. Orville could only shake his head in disagreement. "But they say his spirit is still roaming these parts, in revenge for what happened." He looked around himself as though maybe Messiah Ward was coming over the gunwale right then with a face full of worms and taloned fingers, a groan bubbling up his throat. "Maybe we should go?"

Ned dismissed his friend with a wave of his hand. "Stop being silly and catch some fish, then we can go—"

Suddenly, both of their poles were yanked from their hands—

"What the hell?!" Ned said as he watched his pole disappear into the water and the bugs on the surface dispersing like ash.

A bright orb of light popped on further out in the lake behind them. Orville saw this and tried to make sense out of it. "Hey, what's that?"

But Ned, being a man of common sense, could only respond with what it could naturally be. "That's another *boat*."

Something that could be the klaxon horn of the Devil's bell whined out over the lake, piercing the ears with its vile note.

"Is *it*?" Orville asked, his fingers in his ears, certain this was not *just* a boat, but something else entirely.

Ned was watching, unsure if it was a boat after all. But, being he had absolutely no idea what else it *could* be, and why it was coming on faster toward them, he started waving his hands around. "They don't see us! Wave your arms around before we get run over!"

They both started waving faster, hollering over the din of the encroaching boat motor and that piercing resonation of a horn that sent a shiver up their backs. It was coming on quick, too quick for them to grab the paddle and make a go with it. Instead, they sat there, voices growing scared as the light on the boat became an expanding ball of white fire to their eyes. Before they could blink away at this blinding beam, the boat crashed into their own, tossing them off their seats where they spun in the air a good distance before smacking the water.

Orville was the first one under and the water around him was black and bubbling and deep. Disoriented from the fall, he found himself not in the gentle bosom of a placid lake, but in a tormenting, shadowy expanse of lung-splitting darkness. The water smothered him, pushed against his lips, and found ease into his mouth. Something else was there too. It knifed the surface above him, a black, oblong shape on the surface. Before he could so much as see what it was, his face was caught in a cyclonic fan of edged silver, mulching the meat down to the bone before even that fragmented, whipping his brains out around him in a floating red cloud.

Ned hit and instantly came back up, breaking the surface with a gasp, his red hair flat against his head and face, his jean jacket dark and heavy, weighing him down. He looked around him at the water, concern for his friend's safety on his mind after not seeing him. "Orville! *Orville!*"

Something brushed up his legs and he backed away instinctively while keeping himself afloat. The surface began to boil as a form materialized in front of his eyes. It didn't take a genius to see that it was Orville, but headless, his throat shredded and streaming tissues and blood. Ned shrieked out as he backpedaled and splashed away from his friend's body which seemed to be floating after him even in death.

The sound of a motor somewhere in the dark turned him around, eyes wide and haunted by the night. He saw it before he could scream again. A black boat, sleek and vulpine, dark as the night itself. It made his stomach twist up, his blood go cold just looking at it sitting there like it always had been sitting there, or maybe appeared out of the ether, a manifestation of some kind.

"What are you?! *What are you?!*"

In a flash that startled any further questions, the boat circled him, ringing him as he splashed and cried, trembling and whimpering, Orville's body getting closer. Like a shark smelling blood, vectoring in, the boat came around and swung right over the top of him, the propeller ripping across his body, splitting him lengthwise to separate and yawn as ribbons of intestines and meat spilled out from his shell and blood turned the water red.

4

The lake harbor office wasn't much to look at from the outside by any means. It was small, cramped, big enough to take a step inside, see all there was to see in front of you, and another step backward to be outside. But what more did you really need? It sat on the edge of Lake Jude, over the water itself. Its exterior was a glossy, powder blue, with a white, metal snow roof that came to a thirty-degree peak.

Inside sat a man who was up to his ears with steam over the goddamn computer again. It got his face red as a beet on a skillet and twisted his expressions to those of impatience. After working on the damn thing over the last few months—a gift from HQ —he still couldn't figure the fucking thing out. It was always giving him a hard time like it had some personal grudge against him. Even the simplest of things that most would find easy to push through, would get a glare from his tired, sagging face.

Harbor Patrol Chief Barney Rayl looked over his shoulder at the typewriter sitting on a desk behind him, covered by sheets of paper that looked as old as the damn thing itself. It was those people and their attitude toward accepting technology that forced his hand to upgrade his life to computers—or as he saw it, more problems he didn't need. When they told him they preferred things organized that way, Barney about came unglued, telling them in no uncertain terms, and vocals that could injure an old woman's ears, that he could do the same damn things they wanted from him with the typewriter that he could do with the computer. But they would only smile at him, the smile maybe a young person would give to the elderly before they had to wipe their ass clean for them.

Frustrated by the computer's lack of speed and understanding of his commands, both verbal and physical, Barney slammed a fist down onto the keyboard again, hard enough to shake the clunky monitor with a series of flickering lines. In his late forties, bushy gray hair down around his neck, and a good belly rounding him out, Barney just didn't have it in him to learn all the intricacies involved to become familiar with these modern computers and the like. Why couldn't they leave him the hell alone and let him carry on with the typewriter he'd been cracking at for most of his life? It never seemed to bother no one else.

He waited for the screen to reset itself after the pounding he gave the keyboard.

"Man, I miss the old days." He looked over to the typewriter again and gave a smile that brought him back. "Yes, old technology you can count on!"

The phone next to him rang. He scooped this up with a thick hand.

"Lake Jude Patrol Chief Barney Rayl speaking, how may I help you? What? ... A swamped boat at Lodgers Point ... Probably Ned and Orville's. You know they illegally fish in that spot all the time ... yep, okay, I'll go check it out."

Hanging the phone up, he stretched out his arms

and legs to get the blood flowing, pushed away from the computer, and got to his feet. He fixed his hat to his head and made sure it felt right before hiking his pants trim around his waist.

"If that boat belongs to them, I'll fine them both this time!"

Taking a step away from his desk, leaving that bastard box of gadgets and blinking, winking, funny lights behind, he took the keys from the hook near the door and stepped outside.

Immediately, he was hit with a cool breeze as he made his way down the dock past the multitude of boats moored securely to their pilings. Not a soul passed him by this morning, and seeing as there was only a light amount of folks bobbing around on the lake, it would make his job easier to push his way through them.

Coming to his boat at the end of the dock, he unlatched the rope, tossed it in the boat, and dropped inside. Getting seated behind the wheel, he took the CB from the dash and hit the button.

"This is Barney to HQ, I'm in boat number 7 and I'm heading to Lodgers Point to check on a swamped boat. I'll report in after I assess the scene, but I'm sure it belongs to Ned and Orville. Out."

Hooking the CB back in its place, he turned the key over and let the engine get some juice. After it started up, he reversed out into the lake. Swinging around to face the blue waters that glittered like a vast field of sapphire, he nosed forward, setting the throttle forward, and sped his way across the lake.

Lodgers Point wasn't close to the station by any means. It was at least a fifteen-minute boat ride across the open lake from the dock to the Point at high throttle. But today, he didn't mind at all, didn't mind the escape from the cramped confines of the office and putting some space between him and that goddamn computer. It was such a nice and clear day outside, he was enjoying the openness around him, and seeing the thick stands of full oaks and maples and pines on the white shores and the quaint vacation homes tucked beneath their green and orange and flaming-red canopy. Beneath the sun, the lake was a sharp blue. A slight wind with the smell of pine resin cut across his face with a cool mist blowing over the nose of the boat. It was rejuvenating out there on the lake, under the eye of the warm sun. Unlike the office, which was a stuffy, joyless space with the smell of wet ink and paperwork and old coffee in the air. Being cooped up in the station like he was most days, it was getting hard for him to remember what it was like out there on the open lake. Nothing exciting ever happened around Lake Jude that required his attention for too long, nothing this far out. Sure, there would be the occasional broken-down vessel on the water that he would have to help drag back to the ramps or docks or scoop away some refuse collecting off the shore, but beyond that, it was pretty stale—boring.

But when striper season hit the town every year, the colors on the trees changed and Jude saw an increase in its fishing population and campers. Barney would often have to apprehend those on the water with a little too much drink in their bellies and their tempers and egos inflated. But it never got too violent. He was glad about that. At his age, he just wanted everything to move on with ease. The only thing he wanted to escape was that tiresome paperwork that seemed to pile up every day with no end in sight. Most of which, to him, were useless daily reports of the Lake's upkeep and wildlife, the state of its fish. But being out there on the lake, all those reports didn't mean beans to the man right then. He had a job to do, and he was there to do it.

Lodgers Point was a popular spot for most locals and particularly the visitors to the lake. The only downside to it was that it was off-limits for fishing. It was designated a swimming area. This always got the locals' ire up at the town hall on account the Point was plenty big enough to fish and enjoy a good swim. But there was no debating with the council. You got caught hooking fish at the Point, you were fined, simple enough.

On either side of its shores were rows of bushy oaks and maples, the shores themselves flush with ducktails and reed beds. It wasn't long before he spotted the boat from a hundred feet out as he eased his craft into the Point. From what he could see of it, he knew it was Ned and Orville's right away. It was a small paddle boat with a rusty red paint job with metal trim on the gunwales. It was floating upside down in a bed of reeds, water lapping its hull.

Coming up alongside the pathetic thing, he dropped the throttle on his craft until he was a few feet from it. Standing there with his hands on his hips, he tipped his hat back, examining the boat.

"This is their boat, but where the hell are they?"

Spitting into the water, Barney grabbed a retracting pole from the deck of his boat and hung it out there over the water, pushing it forward and shoving it against the small paddle boat. It seemed to be caught up pretty well on something, probably hung up on some driftwood below, so he put some extra muscle into the jabbing until the thing came loose and flipped around with a splash, bringing a body with it.

"Damn!" Barney shouted, dropping the pole into

the water and nearly falling out of his boat. It took him but a moment to gather himself and look over the edge and at that body. His face scrunched up in revulsion.

The body, if it could be called something so intact, floated there in two stringy halves, masticated down to the femurs and rib basket by what he suspected was fish probably nibbling on him all night. Blood bubbled up from below and soon more pieces of what could only be mats of tissue and flesh floated around the surface. Barney looked away, a shade of green on his cheeks. As he did this, something out there in the water about forty feet out behind his boat caught his eye. It was what most would call a mirage or some sort of trick of the light reflecting off the surface of the water. But it couldn't be, no, because what he was seeing was a legible thing, a vaporous formation of iridescent purple flashes followed by a material design of ... a *black boat*. One that looked almost alien in its architecture. He blinked at this a few times, maybe trying to accept what he was seeing, but the longer he stared, what he was looking at appeared to compress down into a flattening mist that caught a draft and blew out across the lake.

Shaking away this illusion, Barney, again, looked down at the mutilated mess bobbing on the water, felt the green on his cheeks again and his stomach knotting up.

"What the hell happened here?"

Yes, that was the question bouncing around in his head.

First off, it made not a lick of goddamn sense. From what he could make of it, this body looked like it belonged to Ned, but what happened to leave him in this state was a mystery. And where the hell had Orville gotten off to? The two were inseparable.

Surely, he was around here somewhere too. Or maybe Orville and Ned got heated with one another and Orville—no, that was unthinkable. They were like brothers. Closer than most.

But still, the question lingered as did many others. And just what the hell was that out there on the water? He kept seeing it there in his mind, just a projection of mist solidifying into that of a black boat with a wicked hull. Did he actually see that or was it the gruesome sight of the body shifting his mental acceptance around and showing him something to take his mind away from the trauma of it all?

He looked away from the remains and back out there across the water. He shook his head—

The water ruptured below and what came up alongside his boat must have been what was left over from Orville. Chunks of meat and flaps of waterlogged flesh, a shoe with a knob of anklebone, and a scalp—Orville's without a doubt. It was floating there like a bloody, black wig.

All Barney could do was stare down, processing what he was seeing.

Something damn funny is going on here …

The church was a small affair of stone walls climbing with ivy and surrounded by azaleas, lilacs, and bushy pines. From the outside, it was a place that would remind you of some isolated parish you might see in such green and lush locations as Ireland or the highlands of Scotland. It retained that old-world quality in its facade and grounds.

On the inside, its silence was stifled by the raging memories of one man.

Father Thomas.

He was there, on his knees praying at an altar rail. In his head, he was haunted by the flashing, flickering images of the cellar and his actions against the Dark Brotherhood. So vivid and lifelike were these recollections that he could smell the heat of the blood in his nostrils, hear the sounds of the lead rounds ripping through flesh and splintering bone, wet things spattering the wall. He could feel the still-warm bodies on his fingers of those he wrapped away like presents and could see them fading into murky relief beneath the surface of the lake. But there was something else there, not a fleeting glimpse of some dread memory, but something tangible and altogether frightening. Suddenly, the very atmosphere of the church was invaded by a pestilential presence. An invidious shadow rolled over the pews and flooded the rafters, seeming to drift down around him like a black fog. He lifted his head away from his hands as he heard footsteps approaching behind him. Not any footsteps, mind you, but something wet and dripping, bringing with it a charnel smell of violated tombs and wormy earth, the smell of the grave on its breath. A susurration of clogged airways crackling like cellophane was behind him now.

Coming off his knees, he swung around to confront this unholy horror and screamed when he saw the figure in a black cloak garlanded with streamers of lake grass, its face a mask of ulcerated bone crawling with beetles and black sockets squirming with balls of worms, its fingers sharpened knives of bone reaching out to him. He fell back against the rail as it came forward. Its mouth started to open and a black rush of sound like that of a freight train screaming through a tunnel crashed into him with such force that he was taken from his feet, flung back like a paper doll, and exploded into a red cloud of—

Father Thomas jolted awake as if someone was there shaking him. But no one was. It was just him in his car, roused from a nightmare that was all too real. Sweat stood out on his brow, and his face was chalky as a three-day corpse. His fingers were shivering and his hair below the top hat was disheveled and wet. Blinking out of his experience, his hands rubbed at the thick red bristles on his face.

Just another dream is all. You're having them a lot lately, you know?

And he was. Nightly. Sometimes during the day, he would see things that could cause a man to go blind and scream. It was terror living with the figments of, not what he did nor what he stopped, but what was still out there, still *alive* in some sentient manner and growing stronger.

Looking out the windshield, he saw the lake sitting there, a flat blue surface, some grass, and picnic tables just past the hood of his car. Not a soul in sight. But sensing something was amiss that he wasn't seeing, he grabbed his binoculars sitting next to him in the passenger seat and he stepped outside.

Peering through the lenses, he gently swept in a slow, meandering eastern curve until he saw something that gave him pause.

It was Patrol Chief Barney Rayl, standing out there chatting it up with a man in blue jeans and a t-shirt, police tape flapping in the wind around them, all of this by the water and some reeds. He studied them for a moment before sweeping over the lake again. Something wasn't sitting right in his mind. He could sense it much like he could sense the change in the air, in the area.

"It's starting again."

It made sense to him because, since the day he delivered the Lord's judgment, that feeling of encroaching evil had never faded. It hung there just behind and to the sides of him, a veritable curtain of dread. Always there, waiting for him, lurking in his conscience, but more than that too. It was a terrible, brooding, rooting.

That night hadn't stopped it and now it was back, strength renewed, and it had only just begun.

Dropping back into his seat. He set the binoculars down and fingered the newspaper clippings on the seat. Taking these in his hands, he looked over them, and not for the first time either.

"Cult Member Massacre! Brotherhood of Darkness killing spree ends!"

That's what they said, more or less. He browsed over these, having memorized each article, each word. The next one he brought up to his face said in fat, bold print: *"Messiah Ward, Cult Leader, MISSING!"*

Another one met his eyes: *"No Clues in Cult Killings. Police Reveal."*

"Community Glad Evil is Wiped Away!"

On and on these went.

He set them down, took some air in his lungs, and held it there. He let out a long sigh before staring out past Chief Barney Rayl to the lake.

Yes, it was back. And this time, it wasn't flesh and blood threats of cult members, but something beyond, a mechanical evil that felt unstoppable. A dire invasion of the Dark One was imminent.

"After all this time," he said in defeat. "It's starting again."

Out across the lake, far out in the center where the blue waves thrashed like a sea in the wind, and the wind howled over the surface, a boat glided. Not a normal boat. But one that was black with a narrow bow like a blade and cut through the water like blood. It seemed to ripple like a heatwave if you looked at it. And its pilot was something ghostly, smoky, and vaporous. It pressed on across the chop, death on its mind, and would not be fulfilled until the entire lake turned red. Before it faded into a blast of particles on the wind, a sound like the wailing dirge of a funeral bell crashed over the water.

5

Lake Jude was a place that she loved, adored really. She had been coming here for the past couple of years now and could never get over the colors in the early days of fall. The way the trees went from dark to fiery oranges and reds, and the pines were still thick and full and stark in contrast to the flaming tops of those oaks and maples.

Lena swung her car into a parking spot fronting one of the beach areas of the lake. To her amazement, she seemed to be the only one out here, aside from the vendor out there in his small shack. This would do well for her, because when she came here, it was for peace and quiet, not the sounds of bratty little kids thrashing in the water or immature men showing off for all the girls in their tight string bikinis. No, she wasn't about that life. She wanted the sun on her face and crawling up her body and the gentle sound of the water licking the sand.

Grabbing her bag from the backseat, she looped it around her shoulder and started to the beach. It was an amazing day. Of course, she didn't expect any less. On the news they said something about a cold front blowing in at some point, but that must have been a mistake because right then, it felt more like summer. Think about that, summer and fall together, a beautiful fusion.

The sun was out full and there were only a few patchy clouds, nothing to impair the hot glare. In fact, it was so bright, she dropped her bag to the ground and took her sunglasses out and put them on. They were a purple-framed set of Ray-Bans that framed her face well. Lena was an attractive woman, you see. Dark skinned, her crimped dark hair tied back in a bushy ponytail. She was wearing a woolen black jacket over a pair of yellow swim shorts that climbed between her thighs, a blue bikini top, and a pair of green flip-flops.

She walked on past the concession stand, saw a man in there looking bored hunched over a magazine, not paying her one amount of attention. Coming around this, she saw the lake sitting out there, and stopped.

It was everything she remembered it being.

Perfect. Everything about it was right. It was like a portrait, something you would see painted up on a postcard or maybe nailed over a booth in some upscale restaurant. The trees were ripe with their changing colors and a light wind brushed the lake. The pines across the lake were interlaced with the reds and oranges of brush and oaks. It was such a beautiful day.

As she took this all in, she inhaled the scents of the lake and the pine resin in the air. She walked off the path onto the grassy field that separated her from the lake and its sandy white shore.

With each step she felt the springiness of the grass blades and smiled as they tickled her toes. The water rippled like beds of crushed jewels and she walked on faster to get to the shore. Once on the sand, she dropped her bag and continued walking, stepping out into the lake and feeling the water around her ankles. It was warm with a dash of coolness that made it perfect against her skin.

"Nice!" she said, cheerfully.

Coming out of the lake, she walked back over to her bag and reached inside for the blue beach towel she brought along. Taking this, she snapped it open and brought it down to the sand. She took a seat, her arms back out behind her, palms flat supporting her, her legs kicking out and crossed in front of her. Sitting there, just breathing in nature, her skin prickled from the wind blowing against her off the water's surface. It felt so good. Suddenly her phone rang from inside the bag, interrupting the peace. Sighing, she dug a hand around until her fingers found and took hold of it.

Without bothering to look and see who it was, she swiped the green dot on the screen. "Hello?"

"Hey, Lena, how's it going?" the chipper voice said. "You didn't call me this morning—"

"Samantha, hi, I decided to head to the lake early. Making the most of my day off. Are you coming out later?"

There was a pause on the other end before, "I might. Where are you exactly?"

"I'm near Lodgers Point. It's beautiful!"

Samantha's voice seemed to retreat and become serious. "I'd be careful."

Lena smiled like she was sure Samantha was about to play a trick on her. "Why?"

"I just heard on the news the Lake Patrol found a body, or pieces of bodies, near there."

Lena felt a chill up her back. But at the same time, she thought maybe Samantha heard that piece of information wrong, or perhaps it was an altogether different place she was thinking of, a different lake. It didn't seem like anything happened around Lake Jude. It was paradise. The thought of bodies discovered didn't sit right. "Well, you'd never know by looking around," she pointed out. "What happened?"

"A boating accident, I think."

Lena felt relief with that bit of news. Accidents were common on lakes, and bad things could happen quickly. "Well, there you go, nothing to worry about, and I'm going to *swim*, not boat, so I should be fine."

"Be careful just the same," Samantha told her, real concern in her voice now. "That place has a history. I don't know why you don't use *Bonk Beach* instead."

Lena laughed. "It's too crowded there. Lotsa noisy brats and perverted leerers."

"The perverts are the most fun!" Samantha giggled.

Lena rolled her eyes. "Figured you'd say that." Feeling the lake calling to her, the smell of pine in her nostrils, she tried to end this call to get her feet wet. "Give me a ring before you head over."

"*If* I head over."

"Okay, *if* you head over. Maybe we can grab lunch at the concession stand across the way."

"Okay, catch you later. Bye."

"See ya."

Shutting her phone down, she dropped it into her bag and worked herself out of the jacket, tossing it to her side. Her body fully exposed to the sun now, heated fingers of warmth smoothed over her skin as she lay fully back, her hands clasping beneath her head, eyes closed. She listened as the breeze ruffled the trees and the sound of the water lapping the shore. It was all so peaceful and tranquil. After the week she had at work, this was just what she needed. A perfectly relaxing day.

She was feeling the sun baking into her skin when the roar of a motor out in the water raised her off the towel. She looked around her, confused by the fact that she wasn't seeing anything.

"If that's a boat, they'd better watch out for rocks. It's pretty shallow around here."

But something was funny. She could still hear it as though it were somewhere in the distance, but there was nothing there. No sight of anything. One second it sounded like maybe it was right off the shore, the next, a distant memory. She was sure she had heard it. But there was nothing there. No sign of a boat at all. No waves to suggest one tore across. She looked down the lake, following the shore to each side, but again, nothing, just emptiness and the blue glimmering of the lake.

Figuring she was just hearing things, she dismissed the whole thing, got up off the towel and walked into the lake. She was in up to her knees and bent over to dampen her arms and legs with water. She splashed some on her face. Beads of water ran down her breasts and followed the grooves of her flat stomach. She looked up to the sun, and felt the water on her drying instantly—

An explosive wailing sound turned her around and almost took her off her feet with a scream. Sitting there in the water five-feet away from her from her was a boat. Black and polished like an ebony gem. It seemed to hover there rather than float, and misty tendrils spilled over the gunwales, bow, and stern like vapors of black ice.

Her eyes grew really wide behind the sunglasses. "Huh?!"

It was almost too real, but it wasn't. It was there, sitting right there in front of her, seemingly drawn out of thin air or maybe space. She leaned forward, trying to get a peek inside, but that was impossible. The whole thing was dark, so dark it was hard to tell what exactly it was made of. Was it material or something nebulous and shadowy given form?

She had to say something, anything to chase away that awful tingling running up her spine. "Hello? Hey, Asshole! You can't moor your tub this close to shore, and where did you *come* from?"

Looking at that boat was like looking into some forbidden portal into a world the mind could not accept without any amount of logic. It sounded wild, but that was the truth of it. Because she was feeling something downright atavistic in memory. A touch of nightmare and winged demons across the face of the moon, things with red eyes and claws in the woods. It gave her a sense of unremitting terror and horror.

"Well, get outta here then!"

She was standing there, nearly captivated by the streaming vapors and the aura of the thing and hadn't much time to react as its engine roared and the black body spun around, slamming into her like a bear charging a rabbit and flinging her face down on the shore. Pain spiked through her body as her head lifted away from the sand and she saw the propeller cycling closer to her face.

"No! Help!!"

But it was too late for Lena. The propeller wings sucked her in and hacked her into a meaty, bloody spray over the white sand. Pieces of her flinging, bones, and blood misting in the air.

After it ripped its way through her like a wood-chipper with a bushel of twigs, the boat seemingly vanished, leaving nothing behind. No smell of engine oil or gas, nothing but the pungent smell of coppery death and a body butchered to rags on the shore.

6

Back in the station, Barney poured another mug of coffee to the rim, his second this morning. Spooning a healthy amount of sugar into the cup, he gave it a mixing and pulled deeply off it, the steam of it on his face.

He smiled as it got his blood going, softened his thoughts a bit. "That's some good Joe."

He was fixing to take another pull and park his body behind the computer for some paperwork when the phone took him away from the task. Something he was glad for.

"Lake Jude Patrol Chief Barney Rayl speaking. How may I help—*what? Another* body ... but that's three in one day! Where?" He set his coffee down before he dropped it. The way he was going, his nerves were starting to draw tics in the corner of his eyes. "Lodgers Point?" He wasn't surprised. "Close the area off until further notice. I'll be right there."

Grabbing his hat, he took a final pull of the coffee, turned the computer off, and took a walk outside into the sun.

"Dying around here is becoming a bad habit."

Back out on the water now, seated in his boat, he sped across the choppy white caps headed for Lodgers Point, the spray of the lake on his face, the sun beating down on him coppering his arms.

It was funny to him, really. Nothing seemed out of place to suggest anything was amiss; no curious folks reported in the area, nothing but bodies now, and badly mauled at that. And all of sudden like, too, just right out of thin air. Today started like any other day, but the more it dragged on, the stranger it was becoming. Everything appeared normal on the surface. But yet, there was an undertone here. Like a poison in the air building up and slowly pushing over the town. He thought back to that weird, smoky apparition he'd seen on the water when he discovered Ned's body, and the meaty pieces of Orville. It hadn't bothered him so much at the time he saw it, but now that he was thinking about it more since then, it made the hairs on his neck rise and his skin pebble.

As he cruised along, wind blowing over the bowl, the water thrashing, he had a strange suspicion like maybe someone was following him, observing him, watching him just over his shoulder.

He looked out behind him.

Nothing there to intrigue the eye, just the foamy water and the far-off blue haze of the low mountain range. There were a few boats out in the chop now, most sitting in place or trolling along. Nothing too strange there. But this feeling—it was persistent. Like an itch you kept scratching at but it wouldn't go away.

He heard what sounded like a motor starting up near him. He quickly jerked his head around his shoulder, thinking there was a boat coming at him that he hadn't noticed while he was busy thinking.

But again, nothing was there, nothing alarming anyhow. But his hackles, they were still raised as if he were expecting imminent danger.

He increased the speed on the throttle and zipped on, oblivious to the black phantom on his tail, just out of sight, following him like a banner of smoke and particles and weird purple pixelated light.

Pulling into Lodgers Point any other time wouldn't be such a bad thing, but today it irked him. It was like pulling into a crime scene still haunted by figments of the dead. The blood was still there, the prints of the bodies chalked out, the smell of opened organs and voided bowels. This was sacred ground now, a violated place. Even the sun appeared to dim over in this stretch, like a shade had been thrown up over the entire Point.

Reducing the throttle, the wash of the lake water came rolling around the stern as the motor puttered and the boat meandered slowly down into the channel. His eyes searched out the Point where he saw the dense thickets rearing further back and the reeds and cattails poking from the shore and running into the lake. He was reminded of Ned, or what was left of the poor man, roiling up from the water like something unclogged from a gutter, floating there in ribbons in a stain of blood.

He eased the boat alongside the dock that moored the paddle boat and kayak rentals. Killing the engine as he neared, he tossed his rope out to the piling, pulled the craft flush with the deck bumpers and tied her off before making his way over to the scene.

He saw it as he walked off the dock—the white sheet draped over the body in the grass beneath a canopy of oak leaves. The closer he came, he could see something was wrong. It didn't look like a body in the traditional sense, but lumpy and disordered. Maybe a collection of parts, he thought. It must have been really bad considering the sheet was more red than white.

Stepping beneath a band of yellow tape, he saw Bill Tyler, the coroner, standing over the remains, a pencil in his fist, writing things down on a clipboard. He approached him, glancing down at the feet poking from the end of the sheet—both bloody and twisted the wrong way.

Not bothering to lift the sheet to see what it looked like under there, he asked, "Well, what do you think?"

Bill finished with whatever he was writing then looked up at Barney with a flat, emotionless expression on his sagging, somber face. "It's obviously a boating accident," he said as if it could be nothing else. "She got too close to a propeller. Whether it was a hit-and-run, or malicious, I don't know. That's your job."

Barney couldn't figure this one out. This wasn't a job for him. He was supposed to handle small domestic affairs involving the lake, nothing like death and bodies and pieces of them. It was all so boggling to the mind, and so sudden. He couldn't frame what was happening here. As the only real authority around Lake Jude, since the sheriff department was thirty miles east of the park, it fell on his shoulders for the time. A burden he wasn't much caring for at the moment.

"Three boating accidents in twenty-four hours,"

he said, tipping his hat back on his head. "It seems suspicious."

There was no other word for it. Suspicious is right. Something wasn't adding up here. He'd seen a lot of accidents during his time as Chief, and not one of those involved a propeller slicing through bodies with such extensive damage. The way Ned looked when he found him, it was as though someone ran him through with a chainsaw. And Orville, well, he was chopped thinner than meat cutlets on a plate. He had to use a fishing net to scoop what was left of him out of the water and stuff him in a bag. He had no concept of what the body of the woman looked like beneath the cover, but judging from the lopsided mound below him, he could only guess that it must have been bad—too bad for anyone to see.

Bill agreed to an extent, but he was a clinical man at heart. Cold and calculating. This was nothing more than a boating issue. Probably drugs or alcohol induced. "It does happen. When people drink and get into boats, all kinds of stupid happen. It's a bad coincidence, that's all."

You could tell Barney that over and over again, but that doesn't dismiss the fact that deep inside, none of it was sitting right. And if you wanted to keep throwing out simple conclusions with no basis behind them, only speculation, it was only going to make Barney think about it that much harder. He wanted to laugh at Bill, tell him, no, this was something more than a simple accident. This was *murder* in his eyes. But for the moment, he kept that close to his heart.

"The question is," Barney said, chewing on his thoughts. "*Whose* propeller killed her?"

"Excuse me," a deep voice boomed from a stand

of trees and brush. Both Barney and Bill looked over. A man dressed in black slacks, a black long-sleeve shirt with a clerical collar at the neck, and a black top hat emerged from a wall of trees. His face was tough as tanned leather, lined deeply, lacking emotion. He ducked beneath the tape, coming to a stop in front of the body.

Barney and Bill looked at one another, confused by why the man had come from the woods, why he was there now. Barney was glaring at this man. Something was familiar about him.

"Excuse me," he said again, addressing Barney this time. "May I give the poor soul her last rites? No one should die without absolution."

Bill cleared his throat, brought his clipboard to his face, and walked off to leave the Chief and this priest to it.

Barney put his hands on his hips and looked the priest right in the eyes. "A little late for that, don't you think? And just who are you anyways?"

The man's eyes looked sadly down at the body as if there were guilt in that look. "My name is Father Thomas, and the Lord is ready to receive anyone's soul, even after death. May I?"

Barney folded his arms. He still wasn't too sure about this character. The name rang a bell, but still, he couldn't place it. "Sure, go ahead, but be quick about it."

"Thank you."

Barney watched the man get down on a knee, his hands pressed together in prayer, his head bowed. He was mumbling some passages from the Good Book that Barney couldn't hear that well, but it didn't matter to him. Barney had never much believed in a deity or God, whatever name you chose to label it. He was an honest and hard-working man. Nothing more, nothing less.

With Bill bringing his assistant over to wrap up the body, there was nothing left for Barney to do here. Besides, he had other pressing issues. A priest praying over the dead was the least of his concerns. He watched the man a bit longer before taking his leave and heading over to his boat.

Finished with the last rites, Father Thomas stood up, appraised the body once more, and saw Barney out walking on the deck.

"Please wait!" he hollered.

Barney turned around to see the Father walking quickly over to him. He waited for the man to be a few feet away before saying, "I'm not dead yet. I don't need last rites."

"Please," Father Thomas intoned, a desperation in his eyes. "I must talk to you. I have some information that may shed some light on these ... *accidents*."

Barney felt a chill at how the man said that. Like he knew much more than he was letting on here.

"You hesitated," he said, narrowing his eyes. "Why? You don't think these are accidents? Let me guess, the *Devil* did it?"

Without saying another word, Father Thomas scrutinized Barney before handing over something in his hand.

Barney took a step back like the priest might have thrust a knife at him but came back when saw a card in the man's palm. He took this and glanced down at it. *The Old Church*.

He looked up—

Then swung around, searching for the priest. He was gone. Just as quickly as he was there, he was a memory. It was like he had simply vanished. He looked out behind him at the water. Again, nothing.

For a minute, Barney thought maybe he imagined this interaction. Of course, that was silly. He was still holding the card. But … where the hell did he get off to? And so quickly?

"That guy must be a goddamn ninja," he shook his head.

7

Three fingers of bourbon sat in his stomach with a second round on the way. He poured this, took it in his fist, slugged it down, and slammed the glass onto the desk hard enough to leave a crack. Reaching for a folder that was sitting in front of him, one that had been sent his way earlier by Bill, the coroner, he broke the seal open and looked down at the photos stacked inside held together by a paperclip.

One picture was of Ned, spread out on a cold slab of steel, his body drained of fluids and pale as white rubber. Pieces of Orville were taking up space on the same slab, stuffed in a plastic bag twisted at the top like a sack of Halloween candy. And the other picture, the woman beneath the sheet. She had a name this time, Lena. He didn't see her with his own eyes, didn't very much want to, but he was seeing it now. There wasn't much left. Like Ned, she was placed on a slab, pieced together like some hideous jigsaw puzzle, a configuration of morbid anatomy. It made his stomach convulse in waves. He felt the green of nausea press into his cheeks again. He quickly closed the folder before his mind went to sauce.

Pouring another drink, he pulled the bottom clean

and stared at the computer, seeing his reflection in the gray screen, seeing that tic back in his eye. As his mind drifted back to the strange boat-like object he'd seen before, the phone on the desk rang, giving him a startle.

Before he could say anything, Bill, on the other end, spoke first. "Barney, I have the full report if you want to listen?"

Relaxing with a sigh, he said, "I'm all ears."

Bill cleared his throat. "Officially, these were all boating related. In fact, the boys here determined it was the same propeller—"

"Then it's homicide," Barney shouted, pounding his fist on the desk.

"You know what the strange part is?"

Barney almost laughed, because this whole god-damn thing was strange, otherworldly almost, with a touch of sinister afoot. "Other than we have a killer chopping up people on the lake with an outboard motor?"

Dismissing the outburst, Bill said, "The blade marks aren't consistent with any prop on the market. It's completely new, maybe homemade. We're going to keep delving into it—"

"Thanks, you do that."

Barney slammed the phone down none too lightly.

Taking the file folder off the desk, he whipped it out across the office where it fell apart against the far wall in a spray of paper and photos.

"Great … Just *great!*"

For a minute, he was about to storm out, put himself on the lake, and find a killer, hunt the sonofabitch down. Do what he had to do to stop this lunatic and his bloody spree before it spread further inland into the community itself. But something caught his eye as he went to stand and do just that. A small black card at his feet. He picked this up. Ran his thumb over the glossy surface. He thought of the priest, this Father Thomas character that just as suddenly appeared and disappeared at the crime scene like a gust of wind.

I think it's time I had a chat with this Father and see what he's keeping from me.

Stuffing it in his jacket pocket, he poured himself another drink and thought about how he was going to handle this situation. If this Father Thomas was related in any way to the killings on the lake, he would have to approach him with caution. He couldn't just go over there blindly like some detective with a chip on his shoulder. It could be a trap, the way he was looking at it, and Barney wasn't prepared for that.

Draining the glass, he poured another, and another after that.

I'll get to the bottom of this, rest assured I will.

———

Lightning exploded and rain pissed down from the sky, running from the eaves of rooftops and flooding gutters, pounding through trees and inching the lake to rise. Father Thomas lay in bed, his eyes sealed tight but flickering with motion. A flash of lightning washed away the blackness of his room for an instant before darkness absorbed him.

Each thunderous roar outside, each strike of energy from the sky, had him squeezing the rosary beads he kept looped tightly around his fist whenever he slept; a trait he picked up after wiping out the Brotherhood and their black magic years before. In the throes of his rest, he started choking and breathing hard as though someone was drowning him, suffocating him with a pillow, or maybe slitting his lungs open with a blade. Sweat ran off his face in rivers onto his pillow.

In another flash of lightning, he seemed to fall far away into some abyss of shadows where he saw a woman lashed to a pole, struggling with the ropes biting into her ankles and wrists, dressed in a simple nightgown of sheer white cotton, flames licking up from a red trench surrounding her. He watched helplessly and in pain from some outer plane, held in stasis as these leaping flames solidified into crimson swords and began to strike upon her, rending her flesh from the bones in a red shower of blood.

Another star-hot bolt of lightning ripped across the sky, and the scene of the woman's fiery consumption fell away from him, transposed by a hideous nightmare of mutilation and iron cages where victims crouched naked and mutated, filthy in pools of waste and gore.

"No! ... No!" Father Thomas shouted in his sleep, thrashing in his bondage to these images.

In a burst of blinding starlight, he now found himself back in the cellar of the dreaded Brotherhood. But not the same cellar into which he flew like a shadow and dispatched death with hot metal and the fury of a burning soul. Rather a stygian tomb, a necropolis of the dead; a place where slanted yellow eyes floated in pockets of shadows, where the screams of agony laced the air in currents, where bulky and monstrous shapes leered and crawled, where vermin ran in rails of locomotion down skull-strewn paths and corridors. Messiah Ward was there, not as the Father remembered that grim day, but as a ghastly parody of his former self. A devil-faced haunter in a smoky black cloak in which two red eyes gleamed from deep within his hood like incandescent rubies. Crouching before him was his flock, not three this time but a congregation; an endless throng of squirming bodies that stretched a league in all directions, a palpitating sea of larval shapes with a hideous squall blowing from their throats.

Over this mass of evil, Messiah Ward, elevated on a lift of violet and pinkish particles, spoke in a high susurration like the voice of a million hornets, repeating the very words he spoke that day before he slit his wrist to fill the chalice.

"My children, my flock, welcome! We have been gathered here for our final sacrifice, as our Master calls us to a darker place, our shaman has seen it in a vision. We have been prosecuted through the ages for our service to our Lord, burned at the stake by infidels! Now, the time has arrived, for our fiery transition ... do not fear!" The volume of his voice grew to tremendous heights as the ceiling blasted far away into a cavernous black vault of flaming stars and the very floor trembled before rupturing and crumbling into a purple mist that floated and chopped like a violet sea in torrential gales. "DO NOT FEAR! THE BROTHERHOOD OF DARKNESS SHALL REIGN AGAIN!"

A scream tore from Father Thomas' throat as he came away from the nightmare that became more material the longer he remained, nearly rolling from his bed with the effort.

In some region of his mind, he could still hear the voice of that thunderous oration echoing and echoing, driving away his attempts to curb its rising intonation. He fought to control his breathing as a crack of lightning flashed his room a sharp blue. And for one instant, in that flash he—no, he didn't see that. There was not a dark shape standing in the corner of his room where the shadows seemed to thicken. It had to be something else, some distortion of the light. But as the lightning cracked again, a shadowy form flew at him as a claw clamped his throat, the nails of which pierced his neck.

Father Thomas fought in a mortal contest with this murky invader in his home and grappled with the wrist that held its place like a pole of tungsten steel. His heart racing in his chest, a flash of lightning shot the black of the room aside and he saw the face poised above him, a frightening bone mask of dripping carrion, a fat black spider crawling along the scalp before swinging into one hollow socket.

Thomas screamed as he thrust out the rosary into the thing's face like a shield, and it fell back away from him with a hissing shriek.

Realizing the effectiveness of his action, Thomas held out the rosary between him and this necrotic intruder. Its hands slashed at the air in an effort to dislodge that horrible symbol from its face, before giving another shivering wail as he staggered back and crashed through the door of his bedroom.

Staring at the shattered door frame, Thomas fought with the Lord's will on his side and raced after the mutant in black. With the rosary beads swinging out ahead of him in a ward, he walked past empty spaces and down the corridor, hoping that whatever had attacked him had decided it was much better to run than deal with the might of the Lord within his heart.

Rounding into the kitchen, he caught a vague glimpse of smudged black as the back door fragmented like a sheet of glass as the apparition blew its way through.

Father Thomas was quick on the trail, following whatever had attacked him out into the windy blast of the rain outside.

Involuntarily, he took a few steps back as the gusts

drove against him, a powerful force that shoved him physically back onto the porch of his house. Struggling to hold his position in place before toppling over, he saw, on the moon-frosted lake the shell of a black boat roaring over the lake in a wash of foam, a shrilling horn blowing like a demonic conch.

At the moment his heart threatened to reel back from its life, the phone in the house began to ring.

Ducking back inside, he scooped up the phone hurriedly, rain in his eyes and down his face, on his hands. He spoke with a timid, cracking voice. "Yeah? This is Father Thomas—"

"I'm sorry to call you so late," Barney slurred on the other end, the drink heavily twisting his voice. "But we need to talk."

Thomas stared out the ragged portal of his door. "*Yes … yes we do.*"

8

The sun broke over the eastern ridge and flooded over the lake a deep red with a vibrant ripple of silver on the surface from a mild wind. Typically, around this time of the year and morning you would see a high amount of boat traffic on the lake, fishermen lining the shores and docks, lines in the water, and pulling striper and rainbow from the deep.

But there was nothing typical about today.

Something was in the air, a nefarious plot, a poison in the waters. With the murders of three people in the last twenty-four hours with a killer still on the loose, even the most stubborn of men were dissuaded from braving the lake in hopes of a good haul. the lake in hopes of a good haul. In fact, many of those who had plans to spend all weekend in town enjoying the water had packed their gear and headed back to wherever they originally came from. It was too much of a risk to linger in the area with a madman on the loose.

People didn't come to Lake Jude to die in horrible ways. No, they came to have a good time under the sun, fish the lake, sit around campfires, share some stories, pull some beer, and roast some hot dogs.

Dying by mutilation was for battlefields.

Barney topped off the coffee mug, shoved a spoonful of sugar in and gave it a swish, tapping the spoon on the rim before handing it over to Father Thomas.

"Thank you," he said, taking the mug, and instantly taking a sip, not even bothering to blow at it. He was haggard looking. That was the first thing Barney noticed of the man when he walked into the station this early dawn. It was a bit unnerving at first. He had the look of a man on his last breath, a tired and exhausted face, pits under his eyes, and sagging jowls. This was definitely not the same man he shared a brief spit with at the body yesterday at Lodgers Point.

Barney poured himself a cup, dropped two spoonfuls of sugar inside, and took a long sip. He pulled up another chair and parked himself into it.

He took another sip, looking into the priest's far distant eyes, thinking the man was still back wherever he had been that disfigured his appearance. "Okay, Father Thomas, we've been quiet long enough, let's talk. Tell me what you know that may help my case. These weren't accidents we're dealing with. I'm calling it homicide."

Thomas took a moment to find his words, and when he found them, they came out dry as tinder. "And you have every right to."

Now we're getting somewhere. "What's your take on this?"

Thomas leaned back, wiped at his mustache with a thumb. "You want the truth—even if it challenges everything you may understand about the world around you?"

Here we go, Barney thought. *Now he's gonna fill your head with devils and demons, ghosts and phantom bodies out in the wilds, coming out of the grave, rising from the lake in misty, windy sheets.*

He took a sip and prepared for the nonsense. "I wouldn't expect someone in your profession to lie to me. Yes, the truth."

Thomas sat his mug on the desk and took in some air, maybe to clear his head, maybe to prepare this Chief with a lesson that he was sure to dismiss outright before accepting. After all, how could you accept something so abstract and what most people would call, superstitious? "What you are dealing with, what we all are dealing with, is an evil force, and entity that has lived on beyond death. It's here, now."

I knew it. Selling me on witchcraft and goblins and skeleton walkers, just another superstitious Halloween jest is all.

Barney wasn't surprised of course. He would expect nothing less from a priest to admit that what was killing those folks on the lake was some sentient evil freed from the pits of Hell. "What do you mean *we* are dealing with?"

"Yes, *we*. You, because it affects you directly, me because it is by my actions it is here."

The pieces keep falling together. So, the Father might have had a hand in this or knows something close to his heart that could help unlock the true face behind these grisly deaths. "You're not making much sense, Father Thomas."

The priest smirked, but it was anything but nice or full of mirth. It was a twisted grin, like he was showing a side of himself he had tried desperately to keep concealed. "Do you remember the Brotherhood of Darkness incident a couple of years ago?"

Barney drained his mug and poured himself another, this time adding a squirt of bourbon to the mix.

"Of course, that was headline news, but they're long gone, right?"

Thomas kept his lips sealed as his eyes wandered into memory. He was seeing the flash of his pistols thrust into the masked faces of those impish servants of their Leader. He was smelling the cordite around him and the stink of hot blood. He came away, his eyes blinking and wet as chrome. "The massacre ... the disappearance of Messiah Ward, their leader ... I am responsible for that."

Barney stared at this man without blinking. A lot of things were going through his head, but this ... it was almost too much. How could this nice man who had the look of a sweet grandfather to him, be some sort of killer? Barney couldn't imagine him taking the law into his hands, getting blood under his nails. A man of the cloth taking the sword to the iniquitous, in this day and age?

"You were involved in the massacre?"

"Yes!" Father Thomas said, saying it as though a great weight had lifted from his shoulders. His face took on a brighter shade as his eyes turned dark. "I ... and I alone, was responsible for the demise of that death cult." He appeared to lose his strength but for a minute. "Please ... don't tell the police until our work is finished ... I will accept the moral and legal ramifications of my actions ..."

Barney had to hand it to the man. It took a lot, especially for a man of God, to bring mortal justice to his fellow man in such a manner. No matter how vile or wicked they may be. Barney had no intention of speaking to the police. If what this man says is true, what crime was committed here? The vanquishing of a great evil in the community? It's no different than a surgeon knifing out a tumor.

"Well," Barney was saying as he drank his coffee,

feeling the booze back in his blood. "A lot of folks might see what you did as a favor, not a crime—"

"It is what it is," Father Thomas interrupted. "And I will stand before God and answer for my actions ... but they must be stopped again—for all time."

There was more to this than the priest was letting on. Sure, Barney had heard about the Brotherhood, but beyond that, their plans, their origins, all that back-lore, he was left in the dark. "Why don't you start at the beginning, Father ..."

A great pain seemed to descend, to wind around him and sink its talons into his heart. It spoke volumes in his eyes which became mere points of shadow. A purge of all that had worn him down into a spiritual wreck was on the verge of release, a great mental intoxication settled on his mind.

"Messiah Ward was my *brother* ... both men of the cloth. A monster and a fallen priest." He took a moment to collect the timbre of his voice from waning into a fit of whispers. "He, my brother, wanted the ultimate power, the answers to all of life's questions. He became disillusioned with God's work and found what he was looking for in Satan's palm. He enticed others to join him, and soon they were committing despicable acts in his name. I had to stop it before it went any farther."

Thomas could hear his voice as a whisper now as he plunged back into the abyss of that dark history, back into the cellar of shadows. He felt the fabric of the mask on his face, the weight of the guns clutched in his hands; he could smell the blood of the sacrificed in the air.

The shadows were alive and menacing, shaped into leering profiles that cackled as he advanced down a narrow path. Whispers of the damned and far distant harried after him, jumped into his mind with a latching bind that haunted him to this day. But he fought these aural invasions with passages of God's word.

Into the dark ceremony he came, an avenger of God's hands. The pistols leaped with sparks and flame as bullets impacted flesh.

"We've been expecting you," Messiah Ward said to his brother. But not the same Messiah Ward that he killed that fateful day, but the transposition of a demonic form, a towering creature of pebbly black flesh and bulging muscles that stood out in thick black cords, terribly long, hooked claws, and molten eyes. *"Old friend!"*

Father Thomas screamed as he came out of the vision.

Barney felt his heart jump to the sound of that shriek. The air went dry in his lungs, wondering just what had happened to the Father. Somewhere in his speech, he sort of drifted away, like his mind had detached and all that was left was some automaton on autopilot.

He seemed to compose himself after a few sharp breaths. "So, there you have it ... that's how it went down."

Instead of asking what had caused that scream, because he was pretty sure it was a flashback of some kind, much like a war veteran would fall back upon after recalling some hideous experience, he said, "Okay ... assuming I believe you, which I'm not certain I really do—"

"It is hard to swallow, I admit ..."

Barney took a long drink of coffee before continuing. Did he believe what this Father told him? It was hard to bite down on and swallow, that's for sure, but was it unreasonable? After these deaths suddenly? And with the glimpse of that strange, ghostly projection on the water, he was starting to wonder. "What can we do? How can we put this to rest?"

Father Thomas eyed this man as though he had discovered an ally in his fight with evil. "The derelict building at Lodgers Point?"

Barney nodded. "Yeah, we chase partying kids from there at least twice a week."

Ignoring the comment, Thomas continued. "That was their sanctuary. We need to consecrate it so Messiah Ward can never return to it."

"What do you mean?"

Thomas leaned forward, his eyes getting wide. "We must bless it, make it pure again with the hand of God and he will never be able to set foot in there again."

Barney had his doubts, but he was going along with it. It was better than doing absolutely nothing. And who knows, it could set things in motion to put a stop to whatever the hell was really going on. "You're sure about that?"

"Positive."

"And what if we don't find him?"

A smile of victory curled his lips. "He'll find *us*."

9

Most people thought Chuck was funny going scuba diving in a lake. They would ask him, *"What the hell are you supposed to find down at the bottom of a lake?"*

He'd laugh about that, and fire back: *"Well, what the hell are you supposed to find in the ocean?"*

Because most people, when they thought about scuba diving, thought about the sea. Not a lake. But Chuck Barry, he'd been diving in rivers, ponds, a few deeper creeks, and Lake Jude for nearly twenty years now.

You'd be surprised what you would find at the bottom of a lake, he'd tell them. Especially over in Lodger's Point. Why, he found necklaces, bracelets, rings, even once found an old Smith and Weston .44 with a load of ballpoint rusted in the chamber. He'd even come across a few sunken craft further out in the lake. It was amazing, really, the things you could find sitting on the bottom collecting silt. Today, he had already found a watch and an old Nokia cell phone, that, surprisingly, was still functional. He kept those in his go-bag.

He checked the pressure gauge taped to his wrist

and saw he had plenty of air left to breathe. He wouldn't have to come up for a new tank for around half an hour.

Kicking his legs, he glided along a rock bed, pushing aside strands of grass, and digging with his knife in the sand. Nothing to find, he swam on, his fins pumping behind him, bubbles rising out of his regulator, his mask as clear as crystal. Luckily for him, the sun was out full today, and its rays gave him plenty to see by.

He came into a thick forest of grass that rose from the bottom a good five feet in wire-thin tendrils, waving lightly with the currents overhead. He swung his knife out ahead of him, cutting through to avoid being tangled. One time, he had gotten himself tangled up pretty good. He wasn't sure how it happened, but it took him a while to cut himself free the grass. It was almost as though it were alive, moving and slithering around him. He shuddered at the memory. There wasn't a whole lot that spooked him in this lake, but the reminder of that day lived in his head. He should have avoided the forest today, but he worked up his courage and slashed his way through. The bottom fell off down a declivity of darkness. To his eyes, it was a plunge into another world. He had never gone down that far and didn't intend to do so today.

He swung himself around, checked his gauge and compass, and looked up at the grass forest—

Was that a person?

That's what it looked like to him. Like another diver swam past.

It couldn't be a fish, he thought to himself. *Too big.*

Not only was it big, but it wasn't shaped like a fish at all. In fact, it wasn't much shaped like a man either, more like a fog had drifted past, a cloudy expanse. But that made about as much sense as another diver down here, considering Chuck Barry was the only known diver to the area.

Looking around, keeping his breathing steady, he held tighter to the knife and pushed off the bottom, avoiding the area where he saw the shape.

After he pumped himself out of there and stopped looking over his shoulders, he dropped the silliness of the situation and continued with his treasure hunt.

He was coming into the mouth of Lodgers Point now, climbing—using his hands to crawl forward along the bottom—over sediment-caked stones and sand. He didn't want to head too far in because he swept that area yesterday and decided there hadn't been enough time for anything valuable to accumulate in the lake. So instead, he skirted the mouth and stayed where it was deeper and cooler. There was a dip in the bottom, and he slowly climbed down into it, taking his time, his flashlight back in his hand, the beam punching through the water. He spotted something.

Swimming over to it, the closer he got, he saw that it was a crate. A sealed crate at that.

This could be pay dirt! A real find.

It looked old like it had been sitting there for maybe a year or more. Coming to it, he ran his hand over the wood. It was covered in a thick layer of silt that came away from the crate in a cloudy plume. There was a word stenciled in red letters, but he was having trouble reading what it said. Letting the light fall on his wrist, he tried to dig his fingers into the seams but there was no give, nothing was moving. It was locked down tight.

Pulling his knife with one hand, the flashlight up in the other, he shoved the tip into a groove and started working it. He felt it give slight and now a corner popped a notch.

Bingo.

Sheathing the knife, dropping the light again, he grabbed the corner with both hands and pulled. The lip popped and a column of bubbles shafted upwards to the surface. Taking his light and putting the beam inside, a black mass emerged, a shadowy sphere that lifted from the crate, rising above him and shaping into—

Balls. Common bouncy balls you would see in a rack at the toy store. There had to be a dozen now, rising out of the crate, big black and blue beads. He almost laughed. It was funny, really. Here he thought he was finding something worth a coin, but all he found were children's toys.

Smiling with his eyes, he kicked away when a boat tore over the surface just above his head, the propeller only inches from scraping his skull.

Jesus Christ!

He lowered himself, then swung around, trying to find that boat again, but it was like it had just disappeared. There was no sign of it, and surely there should have been some mark of its path, bubbles, or something.

Well, this is too dangerous, I'm outta here.

He started toward the shore which he knew was a five-minute swim from where he was, he kept low, his eyes searching the surface.

What's that?

He was hearing a motorboat. But where the hell was it? He was looking around above him but wasn't seeing it at all. Then something came right out of the murky water not twenty feet in front of him. An oblong shape wide as a Buick and sharp as a spear.

It can't be, it just can't be!

But it was. Oh yes, it was a boat; a black shadow of oil that surged toward him like a black sword point, and when it impaled his belly with the bow and ripped him into a cloud of meaty confetti, he burst like a bag of gore as the boat faded behind out of existence.

10

Behind the wheel of his car, Father Thomas' hands shook as he took a bend into the graveyard, wedging down the narrow cobblestone road. The place looked much different than when he initially came through. Mist hung over the tombs and enveloped the trees, parted in coiling, drifting plumes as they pushed forward. Funny, there was no mist in any other place in town, just this graveyard, a consolidated mass of vapors that had no intention of leaving.

Barney still had a tic in his eye about this whole thing. He hated that he was caught up in this, that the town was supposedly caught up in this, and had even thought about pulling the plug on this operation. It wasn't every day he found himself hunting demons and putting a stop to demonic cults and forces and the like. This was something else for sure. Barney looked over at Thomas, irritation in his eyes.

"You might want to slow it down," he told him. Once they had gotten into his car, the priest tore through the town, even blowing through a couple of red lights and stop signs, nearly clipping a biker as his focus was so far from where they were the whole time. To maybe lighten the situation a bit, he said, "I'd hate to have to write you a speeding ticket."

Father Thomas allowed a thin smile on his hardened face. "I thought your authority extended to the water only."

Barney held his tongue about how he was the *authority* around Lake Jude and all should have known that. "Just slow it down, okay?"

Barney heard some sloshing in the backseat and hadn't noticed it until now. He looked behind him and saw a case of water bottles, a crucifix, and the spine of an old bible sitting back there.

"You just put in an Amazon order?" he asked.

"Our weapons," Thomas stated flatly, back on his objective.

Barney patted his hip which now held a pistol in a leather holster. "I have my weapon right here."

Father Thomas laughed in his throat. "That gun, that piece of iron, will do you no good."

Barney took that in with a shrug. "Either way, it doesn't leave my side."

The lake split open beneath the bow of the stealth-black craft as its pilot, a skeletal ghoul cloaked in shadowy wisps, tore across the choppy waves, directed by the Master to those who dared to interfere with their Lair. Its eyes burned like hot embers deep in a black pit, its hands, gray and withered, eroding to the bone and strengthened only by thin bands of red tissues and blood, held to the wheel as though molded there, a part of the craft itself. On the craft tore through choppy waves, forever looking to feed the One below.

Leaving the graveyard behind, Barney looked out at
the town as it passed by. It had a sullen feeling to it,
almost like each house itself felt the malignancy of the
Brotherhood back, gaining power every hour. People
peeked through their blinds like scared children terri-
fied to see the boogeyman as the car went on by. It
was like a damn ghost town. Lake Jude should be ac-
tive. It was uncanny to Barney. In all his time as Chief
in these parts, there was never an instance like this. It
troubled the mind.

Father Thomas pulled them into a spot in the
shadow of the old cult's haunting ground. They
stepped out and went around the back of the car.
Thomas swung the trunk open and began taking
things from inside, setting them at his feet.

Barney noticed the big cross sitting there by itself,
something carved of solid oak. It looked heavy. "What
about that big cross?"

Continuing to remove items, Thomas said, "That's
our last resort." He indicated some of the things he
was taking with a gesture of his hand. "These will do
in the meantime." Parting the bag which he took now,
he reached in and came out with a bottle, handing it
over to Barney. "You will need to be armed with these
items. Holy water, the quickest and easiest way to
drive away evil." Next, he handed over a cross that
was fashioned from maple or oak branches, set with
twine at its center. "The cross ... evil cannot stand the
sign of the cross. Take a few of each—"

"You're really serious?" Barney asked him, almost
laughing about the absurdity of what the Father was
handing over to him. It was like something out of that
vampire movie he'd seen on television long ago.
Fright ... something or other.

Thomas squared his eyes onto the Chief. "I don't think you understand the magnitude of what is before us. I implore you, heed my advice and stay *strong*—"

"Okay, okay … I'm with you." As much as he wanted to run and maybe get a hold of an actual sheriff to intervene, something inside of him was telling him to follow through. If this was all an elaborate gag to corner him and maybe take him out of the equation for further evil, he was armed with a pistol. So, either way, he would come out of this whole—at least he thought so. "But if all fails, I'm using *my* religion." For emphasis, he pulled the gun from its holster. A Glock 9mm.

Thomas looked at the pistol in Barney's hand. He recognized it as the same one he had used on the Brotherhood. It may have put them bodily down into pools of blood, but they were still out there in spirit, haunting the lake. "We'll see."

Father Thomas led them carefully between junked old vehicles eaten through with rust and strung with cobwebs, along grassy paths choked with weeds and brambles until they came to the back entrance of the building. It was the same point of entry that all the kids used as a way inside. Barney knew it very well and had boarded it up numerous times. But it did nothing to prevent those determined souls from breaking in.

Something was different about the place today. If anything, this was getting outside his comfort zone, but Barney would say it almost looked *deformed* or *rotted* almost. As though some form of residue had worn down the place he remembered. The siding was peeling to the supports, spotted and clustered with strange growths like barnacles. The grass too, it looked like it hadn't seen a rainfall in ten years, but that was impossible considering it was always raining off and on over this area for as long as he could remember. The whole town was a green paradise, but over here at the old derelict building where they now walked in silence, it seemed everything was going to ash.

"The Brotherhood doesn't clean much, do they?"

Thomas glared at him but ignored the question as he led them away from the back door down a side path with weeds four feet high and laced with dense stretches of cobwebs. Barney couldn't remember there ever being such an area. Maybe because it was concealed by nature gone wild. It could explain how he hadn't noticed it before.

"You certainly know your way around," he said, watching Thomas stomp aside the weeds and fell the cobwebs with his hands.

"Stop talking."

After beating the brush down, he reached out and pushed aside a plank of lumber that a quick glance wouldn't have shown you unless you studied it for longer than a minute.

There was a portal of blackness yawning behind it.

Before Barney could say anything about it, Thomas threw the sack over his back and ducked inside.

Barney felt a knot in his belly. He patted the Glock in its holster for support. He had no idea what he was about to walk into, but it made him feel better to have the iron there on his hip. It brought him a reality he was soon to learn would be more than he ever wanted.

Into the shadowy recess, they pushed through walls of cobwebs that Thomas found a length of

lumber and hacked his way through. These were unlike the ones outside in the grass, these were thick,
strung tight, and wired like ten-pound fishing fila-
ment. Nets of the stuff hung overhead, and a couple
of times Barney felt something crawl up his arms and
back. He swatted at things that weren't there, but in
his mind were real.

Thomas walked on with a purpose, swinging the
rod into barriers of silk, breaking them apart where
they fell at his feet like mist. There was just enough
light filtering in through the small windows set into
the high walls of adjoining rooms they passed, to see
—the rooms where the shadows never slept, and
where things scuttled and maybe whispers drifted
from corners and cracks in the walls.

They came into an open room that, like most else
behind them, was congested with shadows and silken
canopies, everything covered in layers of age and rot,
and the smell ... it churned the stomach. It was a
moldering, musty odor, like the interior of a freshly
exhumed coffin that housed a putrescent sack of
carrion.

Maybe to keep his mind away from awful
thoughts, Barney got to thinking other things as he
followed closely on the heels of Thomas. This secret
place has been under the feet of those kids who had
parties above, all this time. It had been here in this
town, a dark and isolated crypt of secrets.

Thomas broke away from Barney who was still
gaping at the dismal rankness of the place, his eyes on
the shadows tucked against the walls. Luckily, there
were spots of sunlight coming through, motes swimming in the beams.

"This is the epicenter of the evil," Thomas said,
laying his things at the foot of a table that had on its
surface a collection of bones and cobwebs strung in

the eye sockets of a skull and weaved over the eternal scream of its mouth. "The sacrifice room of the Brotherhood of Darkness. Few have entered here and lived to tell about it."

Barney swallowed that persistent knot in his throat and felt sweat on his face. "Well, it's not much to write home about either way."

Thomas kicked over the altar table that Messiah Ward had used during his oration two years before. Taking it and turning it upside down, he placed his bible there along with the rosary. He cracked open the book and started reading lines out in his head, keeping quiet about it.

Barney was standing there, getting nervous, feeling the fruitlessness of that cross and holy water in his hands, and wanting very much to cast them aside and draw out his pistol. In his head, there were things down here watching him from just out of sight. He could feel it. And never once had he felt something so powerfully in control over his fears. It made his stomach twist and heart race.

"So, do I just stand here and look pretty?"

Thomas looked at him with a face that could have been that of a flat stone with painted eyes and scribbled mouth. "Be fortunate you haven't been called on to do anything ... yet."

Barney felt his skin crawl again. "I don't like the way you said that."

Shutting down any further small talk, Thomas got to work.

He took out a bottle of holy water and started flicking out beads of the stuff around them. Splashing some on the table where the bones sat, a terrible peal ripped through the room and Barney almost fell over as it staggered his heart. He held tighter to the cross as Thomas continued in his ritual without concern for the demonic tones flying around them.

"Oh Father in Heaven, hear my prayer! I place myself at the foot of Your cross and ask You to cover me with your Precious Blood which pours forth from Your Most Sacred Heart and Your Most Holy Wounds!"

Barney couldn't keep himself from looking around and noticing that it seemed the shadowing of the room had become a moving, thronging body of animation. It started pouring toward them. He swung his cross out a little and it seemed to hold its advance.

"Cleanse me, my Jesus!" shouted Thomas. "In the living water that flows from Your Heart. I ask you to surround me, Lord Jesus, with Your Holy Light!"

Pounding overhead brought Barney to a crouch, one hand going for the Glock, the other firmly on the cross. He was hearing things now, the sound of chattering skulls and bones beating against drums of human hide. Whispers rose and fell.

"Heavenly Father, let the healing waters of my baptism now flow back through the maternal and paternal generations to purify the evil line of Satan and sin. I come before You, Father, and ask my forgiveness for myself, my relatives, and my ancestors, for any calling upon powers that set themselves up in opposition to You or that do not offer true honor to Jesus Christ!"

Barney felt the ground beginning to shake and saw the cracks splitting the foundation of the walls. For one moment, he thought he heard things clawing beneath his feet. But that couldn't be because the only thing there was dirt and bedrock. Unless—

"In Jesus' Holy Name, I now reclaim any territory that was handed over to Satan and place it under the Lordship of Jesus Christ. By the power of Your Holy

Spirit. I bind all evil spirits of the air, water, ground, underground, and netherworld. I further bind, in Jesus' Name, and all emissaries of the satanic head-quarters and claim the Precious Blood of Jesus on the air, atmosphere, water, ground, and all their fruits around us, the underground and the netherworld below!"

Father Thomas felt the stirrings around him, saw the condensing of the shadows, could hear the rustling of feet dragging in the dark, the scrape of claws below.

"In the Holy Name of Jesus, I seal myself, my rela-tives, this building, and all sources of supply in the Precious Blood of Jesus Christ! In the Holy Name of Jesus, I break and dissolve any and all curses, hexes, spells, snares, traps, lies, obstacles, deceptions, diver-sions, spiritual influences, evil wishes, evil desires, hereditary seals, known and unknown, and every dysfunction and disease from any source including my mistakes and sins. In Jesus' Name, I sever the transmission of any and all satanic vows, pacts, spiri-tual bonds, soul ties, and satanic works! In Jesus' Name, I break and dissolve and all links and effects of links with the dark grip of Messiah Ward, his follow-ers, and any resonant blackness they have left behind! In your name, bind it, and make it so. Amen!"

As suddenly as those awful, nightmarish sounds and shapes began, after Thomas' words, they ended. All sound had ground to a silence that was almost too much with the way Barney's thoughts were going right then.

Again, Barney tried to put some light on the situa-tion, maybe to correct his head and shake loose some of those sounds that were lingering in his ears. "That's it? I thought it would be—" he looked around himself before continuing "—more dramatic."

A rushing sound as of thousands of hornets suddenly filled the room, swirling around them. Thomas and Barney swung around, anticipating the source to come.

Barney felt his skin start to crawl all over, his hair going straight, the tic in his eyes flickering. "What the hell!?"

"*Hell*, is exactly what it is," Thomas assured him.

Barney had enough of this voodoo bullshit.

It was time to put some reality into the situation. He couldn't stand around here and let this spiritual hokey get the best of him any longer. He dropped the cross and bottle and whipped out his Glock. Just in time too, because something came out of a shadow. But not a ghoul as one would suspect, nor some demon or fiend, but a man in a dark cloak with a skeletal mask. He was walking toward Barney like he needed a hug. Barney raised his piece and clipped off five shots that flew right through the man as though he was never really there.

"It doesn't die!" he shouted incredulously over the horrible buzzing ringing in his ears, in his head.

"You can't kill that which is already dead!" Thomas warned the chief.

Firing off another few rounds into the projection and around him, he shouted, "Now what?!"

"We use *God's* weapons!"

As he said that, a new shape came winging out of the dark and grappled with Barney, knocking the pistol from his hand. Struggling with this thing, fighting back all he could, he managed to find some space and shoved the thing away enough to reach down and take the cross in his hand. Getting a good grip on it, he brought it up like a blade, and impaled the blackened creature in the chest. It howled as the wood ate into its body, sending it thrashing off into the dark where Barney watched it fall apart like a bursting sack of sand, dusting the floor beneath.

Thomas felt a pair of claws pierce into his shoulders and was pulled back into the dark. A vaporous arm hooked around his throat and began to drag him further into the stygian grotto the cellar now was.

"A little help here!?" the priest shouted, choking out the words.

Maybe in another life, Barney would have run away after seeing all this, but now he was invested. He saw the ghostly figure die, to fall away like foam and scatter after the cross slotted its breast. So, now there was a way out of his madness, a door.

Throwing himself into the fray with Thomas and his captor, Barney tried to pry the thing's arms away. It was a struggle. The thing was adamant about its grasp, it would not let go and where it was determined to drag him, he had no idea. Keeping his eyes peeled for more of them, both he and Thomas fought on until the priest shouted over their grunts, "Break away from it and use the holy water!"

It sounded logical to him. Leaving Thomas to his battle, Barney fell back to the water he dropped, when more of those shapes came out of the shadows, and several seemed to emerge from the floor without so much as a hole for proof. Quickly running back, his heart out of control and near to bursting, he popped the cap on the water and sprayed the figure behind Thomas, instantly sending it back in a cloud of red smoke.

Both Thomas and Barney now began hurling out drops and spraying water at the enclosing horde in front of them. All these phantoms were instantly washed away into clouds of fine, red ash, others exploding in fiery particle showers.

After cleansing what had come for them, and

probing the shadows with their widened eyes, Father Thomas shouted. "We have one more task! *Quickly!*"

Barney had no idea what the next move was, but he followed after Thomas as he took off, back the way they had come. They ran on with the pursuit of whispers close on their trail. They hurried, both of them exhausted by it all and maybe a few years grayer up top. They came out into the sunlight and Father Thomas raced off to the car. He swung the trunk open again and grabbed the heavy oaken cross.

Barney watched on as the priest came back to the door and laid the white plank board back over the opening before placing the cross against its surface. To Barney's astonishment, it seemed to hold as solidly as if he had nailed the damn thing into the board.

They stood shoulder to shoulder, hearing things beyond that door sizzling like maybe they were frying as they got too close.

Suddenly, an eruptive shriek that all but took the ghosts from both of their souls rang out behind them. They turned to see.

"*Messiah Ward!*" Thomas said.

Yes, Messiah Ward in his black cloak, a ghoul now, his face a Halloween mask of fangs and red eyes. A flash of light seemed to mark his appearance as quickly as another saw him vanishing into a murky cloud of smoke.

After the vapors cleared and their hearts went down a notch, Barney looked Thomas in the eyes, a new believer to the faith. "You know, up until now I thought you were full of crap. But now I'm inclined to believe you."

Father Thomas nodded. "Messiah Ward will no longer be able to enter this structure and defile it with his evil." Again, he made the sign of the cross he had been doing since they set foot on these grounds.

"This Messiah Ward character," Barney spat. "He sounds as if he isn't going to take this too lightly."

"Now he can only roam the lake waters," he said with a bit more strength than he had before. "We have made a small victory, but he still has the upper hand."

Barney didn't like that, no sir, he didn't like that at all. "I don't like how that sounds very much."

With a final gaze at the cross that held the building forever under the sway of the Good Lord, they hurried back to the car. Thomas pulled away in a rapid spin, heading to the lake. And Barney, he wasn't thinking about speeding tickets anymore.

It didn't take them long to arrive at Lodgers Point. The way Thomas was driving, Barney expected the man to keep on driving into the water. But they pulled up to the shore and Thomas helped himself out of the car and took a stroll until he stood on the bank, searching out over the lake.

In the distance there was a sound like a boat sweeping through, but there was nothing there, no boat, no ripples. It wasn't in their heads, but there was no seeing something that was purposely kept concealed.

Thomas sighed, his heart heavy, burdened by it all. It was going well, but there was more to do before the evil could be fully purged from this land.

"What's wrong," Barney asked him, feeling the grave weight on this man's shoulders. "He at least has to stick to the water. We'll have another chance."

The priest looked over the lake, haunted by the motor purring somewhere close by. "I'm tired, my friend."

"Well, this is what you were called to do, right?"

"In seminary," Thomas started. "We read and are taught about evil, but it is only in a basic form. What we are facing is more than any head Diocese could bear to battle."

Barney could understand that, but at the same time, they took on those creatures and they were breathing still while those things were added to the dust on the floor. So, there was a way now but maybe some extra help would do good. After all, if Messiah Ward had the power of the devil himself working through him, then maybe holy water and crosses weren't worth beans.

"Can we get help from the church? You know, an army of spiritual warriors or something?"

Father Thomas shook his head in rejection. "I'm afraid not."

"Why?" Barney asked, genuinely concerned. "You guys do exorcisms and stuff like that. Why is this any different?"

The Lake Patrol Chief just did not understand how these things worked. It pained him. "Because to ask for help, I would have to reveal my actions, and that is an even greater evil in the church's eyes."

"You did them a favor!" Barney was astounded, why should the church give two shits about an evil cult falling to blood by one of their administrators of the cross?

"Murder is murder in God's eyes. There is no distinction."

Barney felt sickened by that. Here they were, fighting something God should be intervening in, and they would be blamed unjustly for doing what was needed. What was right. He had to say something to the priest to lift his spirits so they could bring the ultimate battle to this creature of the abyss.

"Well, maybe you have God all wrong."

Thomas looked over at him. "How so?"

"Maybe, just maybe, it was in his plans for you to

be the advocate for good and erase this mess, despite what you had to do."

Some spark jumped in Thomas' eyes. "You think it was God's plan I murder Messiah Ward and his acolytes?"

"*Erase*—not murder—*erase*, Father Thomas."

Thomas allowed a lessening of his facial muscles, going lax with a smile. "Maybe you should have been in the clergy."

"Nah," Barney waved with a hand. "I swear too damn much and drink beyond my fill."

"We all have our vices ..." Thomas said, thinking deeply. "Let's go. We are safe, for now."

Back to the station. But this time, there was no suspicion of what was taking place. The two had formed a solid bond during their battle with the shadowy forms and now they would see this through. As soon as they entered the station, Barney poured himself two fingers and tossed it back, quickly re-filling another.

Thomas on the other hand, was locked in mental combat with all that had transpired, walking back and forth. It was rough going. What had happened was good, sure, but there was still the threat of Messiah Ward out there, the threat of his *brother*. It was all so much pain for any one man to handle.

"Your pacing back and forth is making me dizzy," Barney said, his nerves strung like a bowstring. "Sit down and let's figure out what our next move is, together."

Thomas parked himself in a chair. Topping off a shot, Barney pushed it over to the priest. He took it in his fist and studied it before slugging it down and then asking for another. Understanding the frustration the man was feeling, Barney was all too happy to oblige. Thomas took the second shot and swallowed it down, coughing as it burned its way into his belly.

"Easy on the sauce, boss."

"Another, *please*, to clear my head."

"And soak your soul," he says, topping off another.

Barney waited until the priest's eyes came back around in his skull before speaking. "Since the boating barbarian is relegated to the water, how can we send him to the bottom for good?"

Thomas coughed. "Send him to the bottom."

"Well, yeah. But look at Messiah Ward as a vessel. To disable a vessel, you scuttle it or send it to the watery bottom."

Thomas was pretty sure that is what he said in the first place, but he added, "Excellent thought. That would make a good sermon. If you were to scuttle a vessel, how would you accomplish that?"

The solution was easy for him. "Puncture its hull, burn it, blow it up. They all would work."

Offering the glass out there for another fill, Thomas said, "But Messiah Ward could escape; not go down with the ship."

Barney stewed no more than a few seconds on that as he poured the drink. "Possibly … wait, when you put the cross on the door earlier, couldn't we do the same to Messiah Ward?"

Made sense to Thomas. In fact, it made all the sense in the world. "Lash a cross, a large one, to him, and send him to the bottom." He slammed the drink. "Yes, it would work. Embraced in the sign of the cross, he would be put to an end!"

Barney dropped another slug. "He just isn't going to let us tie a cross to him and dunk him in the lake."

"No ... but we'll figure something out. Spontaneity—that's our upper hand."

Barney smiled. "Just like that?"

"Have faith," Thomas told him, his words a bit slurred.

Barney washed that in his head for a moment. "I think I'll have another drink instead."

Pouring a drink for both of them, Barney slid the Father a glass and raised his own. "To the demise of the Messiah!"

12

Danielle and her boyfriend Mike had taken her daddy's pontoon for a spin when the sun was low in the west. There weren't a whole lot of folks on the lake, and to them, that was a good thing, because what they had in mind required privacy. Tammy and Gregory were there too, unfortunately. All of them were in their swimsuits.

Danielle had long black hair down her back, a yellow two-piece that fit tight to the skin. Mike had a pair of white trunks with blue stripes down the hip. Tammy was more self-conscious and had a black one-piece that covered up too much in Gregory's eyes. Like Mike, he was wearing a pair of trunks, light green with black rings near the knees.

"How many beers have we got left?" Mike called out to Gregory who was currently pissing a stream off the deck into the lake.

"Shouldn't you know?" he asked him, chugging the last of his own brew and tossing the can into the lake.

Tammy opened the cooler. She started counting. "Looks like we have seven left."

"Seven!" Mike shouted, dropping his arm from

around Danielle, leaning forward, his face red from drink.

"I think you had enough already," Danielle told him.

"I haven't had enough!" he countered. "Come on babe, let's turn this tub around and go to the concession stand."

"I think they're closed," Tammy said, her legs crossed—crossed tightly because Mike couldn't stop looking between them.

Gregory pulled his trunks up and dropped next to Tammy, hooking an arm around her shoulder, his fingers brushing close to her breast. "Yeah, dude, they're closed for the night."

"And?" Mike asked. "Who gives a shit? The beer is still there, and the night is still young."

"What the hell are you thinking?" Gregory asked Mike.

"I'm thinking …" and he was at that. It took him a moment to gather his words. "I'm thinking we head on over there and I'll find a way inside and get us some more brew."

"Not going to happen," Danielle said.

"Why the hell not?" Mike asked, pulling his beer, streams of it running down his chin down his chest.

"Because if my dad catches us on this boat, I'm *dead*—and so are you. You know he doesn't like you. And if Chief Rayl catches us—"

Mike started laughing. "That old hog? He couldn't catch a cold!"

"I still don't think it's a good idea," she affirmed. "Besides, we're all underage here. If any of us get caught drinking, much less breaking into a place, we're looking at jail. Does that sound *fun* to you?"

Mike looked at her but what she was saying

wasn't ringing notes with him. "Uh … yeah, sure —Greg, my man, toss me another beer!"

Gregory sat forward and reached into the cooler, grabbed a brew, and tossed it over to his friend.

It sailed past Mike and splashed in the lake.

"Goddamnit!"

"Oh, relax! It's in the water, go get it," Greg laughed.

"You get it!"

"*I'll* get it," Danielle said, tired of these two.

Looking at it now, it was such a big mistake to borrow her dad's pontoon. She had a feeling he would find out and she would be in serious shit. But Mike hounded her until she would agree to it. He would tell her, *babe, it's only for a few hours, and besides, he's away for the weekend. You have the whole house to yourself. Who's gonna know?*

I will, she told him.

But that wasn't good enough for him. He coerced her like he always did, with his eyes. With his good looks and smile. She melted at that smile. She agreed to it but now was regretting the hell out of it. With Mike drunk, and Gregory getting there, it was not turning out how she imagined it would.

Gregory and Tammy were a last-minute thing. It was Mike that invited them. Danielle was just hoping it would be the two of them, because then, she knew, Mike would be less of an asshole. He liked to show off around his friends, and somehow lost a few brain cells in the process.

Danielle took a fishing net and reached out there until the green netting swallowed the can. She brought it up and dumped it on Mike's lap.

"Damn, that's cold, babe!"

"Should have caught it," she told him.

Tammy smiled.

Gregory laughed.

"So, what are we doing besides drinking out here tonight?" Tammy asked.

"Good question," Mike said, popping the beer in his fist. "I say we see how fast this boat goes."

"No—" Danielle said sternly. "We're not doing that. If something happens to this boat, I'm dead. This is my dad's boat, and we're not going to do something stupid in it."

"Oh, come on, babe, just for a minute?"

"*No*, Mike," she said, her eyes daggers into his own.

"Oh, looks like Mike is getting beat down by his girl," Gregory laughed.

"Shut the fuck up!" Mike said, coming off his seat, beer down his chest.

"Chill out, you two," Tammy said.

Mike sat down and drained his beer some more.

Danielle felt the wind blowing into them now. It was getting chilly, and the stars were beginning to come out, winking over the water that was dark. The hills could be the backbone of a black monster in the distance. What light there was left gave everything a hazy, surreal, grainy texture. The smell of fall was in the wind, pine and maple flavors. It smelled great, that is until Mike let rip a burp that took that majestic nature and polluted it with hot barley and gas.

"Oh God, I can smell that over here," Gregory said, his face scrunching up.

"I need to go to the bathroom," Tammy said.

"So," Mike said, his hand pointing to the water. "Then go."

"Out here?" she said, incredulous at the notion.

"Yeah, why not?"

"Maybe because you'll watch her, you perv,"

Danielle said to him, aware of the glances he was giving her.

"Look, Tammy, I'll cover you," Gregory said. "The *perv* will turn around," he said to Mike.

"Why would I want to look at a chick taking a piss? What kind of weirdo do you think I am?"

"One of the worst," Gregory told him.

"Yeah, well, throw me another beer before your lady hangs her ass over the side, will ya?"

"Don't you think you're drinking them too fast?" Danielle asked him.

Gregory tossed him another, and this one he caught. He popped the top. "Not fast enough!"

While Mike and Danielle kept their argument out of range of their friends, Gregory was helping shield Tammy as she slipped her bathing suit down. Not one to pass up on an opportunity to see his girlfriend naked, he watched her undress. Her body was an alabaster that glowed in the night.

"Get a good look?" she asked him.

"Always do."

"How am I supposed to go?"

"That door there," he said, pointing to a small hatch-like door on the stern. Just open that and squat down on the wood deck out there. The lake isn't moving much, you'll be fine."

"And if I fall in?"

Gregory giggled. "Then I'll dive in and rescue you!"

She walked out there carefully, looking down into the water which was black and silvery by the moon overhead. Holding steady to the rails of the back, she lowered into a squat and felt the relief streaming out of her. A motor grumbled somewhere behind her, and this caused her to get flustered.

"Tammy!"

She lost her grip and toppled over back into the lake, naked to the toes, her bathing suit floating on the surface.

Gregory wanted to laugh. Oh, boy, he wanted nothing more in the world. He could still see her face, the way she got scared when she heard the boat in the distance, and the scream that wasn't so much a scream as it was air as she flew back into the water.

"What are you smiling at?" she asked him angrily, her blond hair pasted to her face. "Was that *funny* to you!?"

"No, I—" Gregory laughed. "Okay, I'm sorry, it was kinda funny. Are you okay?"

"Like you care!"

"What happened?" Danielle said, standing behind Gregory with Mike now.

Gregory tried not to laugh about it. "She was pissing, man, and she, well, she fell."

"Yeah, because of a boat!"

"What boat?" Mike asked, staring down at her breasts which were visible just below the water.

She turned around. "That—"

"I'm not seeing anything," Mike told her.

"Me neither," Danielle said. "Did you see one?"

Tammy looked around. "I—I could have sworn I saw a boat!"

Gregory looked over the lake. "Nothing there now."

"Help me up, damnit!"

Mike was getting ready to lend a hand when Danielle stopped him. "I don't think so."

Smiling at her, he grabbed her up by the legs and held her in his arms. "Oh, come on, babe. You know I only want you!"

She didn't believe that one bit.

"What's that?" Tammy and Gregory said behind them.

Mike and Danielle turned to see what they were all seeing. A blinding beam of light growing stronger and brighter, the sound of a motor coming at them, growling in the water like a creature of the deep. It got close, too close, and they all started freaking out and screaming.

"*Watch out!*" Gregory said as the boat, because that's what it was, a black, stealthy missile of death, tore through the pontoon as if the whole thing were made of dry twigs. It exploded in a fireball, sending all of them spinning into the water.

They breached in gasps. Danielle watched as the flames consumed her daddy's favorite party boat, dragging it down into the water, where it steamed as black smoke rolled in a high mushrooming plume.

"HOLY SHIT!"

It was Gregory and Tammy, both screaming together.

Mike, who was treading water beside Danielle, watched on in horror as their two friends literally exploded into bloody fragments. Body parts rained down around them, and a foot and hand slapped Mike in the face. Danielle was sprayed with brains and blood. A clap of thunder, no, of a bomb, no—not a bomb, but a scream, a terrible, demonic bellow rising from the very grave blew across the lake through the red shower of their friends.

"What—*what is this?*" Danielle screamed, her face a livid gore mask.

Mike was looking around, past all the smoke. "I don't see anything—"

By the time they saw it coming out of the smoke— no, a part of the smoke, forming into a rail of purple and red fire, barreling at them, cutting through the water like a flaming torpedo, it was too fast to avoid. Mike ducked beneath the water and the boat, piloted by a devil-faced grinning ghoul, smashed right through her head, where her once pretty face flared up and stuck to the bow in a sticky smear. Danielle's body slowly sank from sight beneath a welter of pooling red.

Mike breached with a scream, choking on water. "Danielle! *Danielle!*"

She was gone.

"Fuck this!"

Mike started swimming, swimming as if his life depended on it, and it did. Yes, it did very much. Having swum in this lake all of his young life, it wasn't so bad for him. At least, it wouldn't have been, but the drink took his effectiveness down a notch.

He was struggling, his arms heavy, his feet kicking out behind him. He was watching his flanks, turning glances over his shoulders. The boat was nowhere to be seen.

Keep swimming, just keep swimming. Someone must have seen the explosion!

He was a far from the shore. At the center of the lake, he had at least another quarter mile to go. With the way he felt, seeing what he was seeing in his mind, hearing the screams of both Gregory and Tammy before the boat blew right through them, it was wearing him down.

Off to his right, he could hear a motor, it was slow, like a trolling motor, soft and deep. He stopped swimming and looked over. It was darker now. There was nothing much to see except a stretching blackness.

Keep swimming, he told himself.

Now on his left, a flash of black flew by like an osprey over water, but bigger, a great shadow of death. He started whimpering in his throat, his arms getting heavier. He could see lights so far away on the shore, and they seemed further the more he swam. Behind him now, that motor, only it was loud as a boiling storm just overhead. He screamed and turned, and saw—

He couldn't tell you what he saw with any logical input. It was a black boat, sure, but it was grainy as if it were an old image from a decades-old black and white film. It didn't seem to float on the water as it seemed to drift to him, a cloud of darkness in the shape of a boat. Below its bow was a purple crackling of fire and sparks, and all around it was a mat of smoky black tendrils that whipped around with violent strokes. And the pilot, its face ... red eyes leered into his own and a grin crammed with fangs grew to impossible width as the boat came forward, missing him by inches. And for one moment, he believed he had been spared, but then the pilot, who now reached over the side with a red-hot sickle, slashed into Mike's face, sending the top of his skull off into the distance on the wings of brains and blood.

13

It took them all night, but they had taken care of what was required of their fight against this dark Messiah. With blisters on their hands, sweat on their brows, they had put together a most crude design hacked freshly from the decapitated limb of an oak tree that had taken a bolt of lightning the night before. To Thomas, this was a sign of God bestowing to him a vengeful weapon of light to wield against this insidious invader from the Red Gulfs below. They shaved it down crossed it with twine. To reinforce its strength, Thomas soaked it in a tub of holy water for hours. He figured they could use all the help they could get.

While Thomas went about his heavenly duties, preparing himself for what was coming, Barney was topping off magazines for his pistol. It might have had no effect on those shadowy forms, but the very notion of it on his person, was enough to give him the boost he wanted—that he needed—with him to help carry him along in this fight to come. In addition to the Glock, he brought along a backup pistol. Just in case.

As the sun crowned its rim in the east, Thomas and Barney walked out to the docks, fully loaded down with their equipment, with their weapons, with their spirits in tow. While Thomas had the usual assortment you'd expect of a priest in his fight against evil, including bottles of holy water, extra crucifixes, rosaries and his bible, Barney brought his wits with him and two pistols fully stacked with hollow points. Not to mention the fifth of bourbon tucked in his back pocket.

Barney stepped down into the boat, taking the bag from Thomas as he followed. Settling behind the wheel, everything in place, he looked over to the priest who had a nervous look to his eyes, in his movements.

"Are we all set?" he asked him.

Thomas nodded. And quietly, he said, "God be with us."

As he crossed his chest with the Holy sign, Barney backed them out of the docks and swept around and headed off out into the lake.

Like the past couple of days, all had taken on a very grave emotion to it. The sky was darker even with the sun peeking on the lake. The very air was permeated, plagued by the *Evil* alive in the waters. The water itself had lost its rich blue complexion, altered with a blackness dark as India ink. It made you feel sick looking at it, wondering what was following you beneath.

Though the lake was absent human life, they could feel eyes on them, watching them. The air compressed with the space of another near them on the verge of leaping out and absorbing them. It got their hearts going, their skin tight as snare drums. It was electric, this feeling. Palpable. Terrifying.

After they went a ways out into the lake, Barney slowed the throttle. "Let me guess," he said, keeping his eyes on the lake. "I know I don't need to ask this at all, but he'll find us, we won't find him?"

It was true. Messiah Ward had been in their shadow the entire time they got on the lake, waiting for the right moment to strike.

"Precisely," Father Thomas said, fingering his rosary beads nervously. "Keep your eyes peeled. He'll be particularly foul now that we robbed him of his dwelling place."

Feeling better if Thomas could put his eyes farther out there in the lake, he handed him a pair of binoculars. "Here, take these."

"Thank you."

Barney watched the priest as he put them to his face backward. He should have laughed at it, but there was no laughter right then in his voice. Helping the priest out by pointing for him to turn them around, he said, "You don't get out much, do you?"

Feeling embarrassed, Thomas said nothing and watched out over the lake.

Jed switched the television off after listening to the news anchor flap his jaw for longer than he should have. It was the same shit the whole time and had been for the last couple of days. *Something funny is going on, it's striper season, blah, blah, blah.* Jed had an earful and decided he needed a bellyful of beer instead.

He walked over to the fridge and looked inside. "Radcliff," he called out. "Where's the rest of the beers?" Behind him down the hall of their trailer, he heard the toilet chug a load down into the pipes.

Radcliff, a man of about fifty with short dark hair and glasses dressed in a pair of dark jeans and a white t-shirt came down the hall, fixing his belt.

Jed got a whiff of what his friend brought along behind him. It stung the senses and made you want to puke or maybe set fire to the place. "What the hell died in there?" he said, waving his hands in front of his face.

"Shut up, man!" Radcliff told him, squeezing behind him. "The beers are on the bottom shelf. Open your half-baked eyes and look!"

Seeing them sitting in the vegetable crisper, he reached forward. "Oh, thanks." But still that smell was coming at him, smothering into his lungs, changing his blood type. "God, the smell from your crap is so bad I'm going outside, Jesus Christ."

As Jed took off out the door, Radcliff waited there and got a smell of himself and the air. After a second, it attacked him, that smell winding around him with feculent spores that were enough to scrape away with a spoon. He pinched his nose and ran outside.

Jed was around his friend's age; a couple of years shy of fifty. He was wearing a red and orange plaid long sleeve shirt and a pair of blue jeans. He took his spot in his chair and popped the can on his brew, staring out at the lake which was only thirty feet from their porch. It was the perfect placement. Both were heavy fishers of the lake, and they had the best access point. The trees were gold and red fire around them, and a breeze whipped through. If it wasn't for that funny feeling hanging like a pall over the town, it would be so damn perfect.

Radcliff came out with his jacket on and plopped down into his chair. He took a pull from his beer and put his eyes on the lake.

Without so much as a warning, a black boat materialized in a sparkling, violet outburst of particles, sitting there right on the shore.

Radcliff almost dropped his beer, something that was a violation between the two of them.

"Hey Jed," he said. "Do you see that!?"

"See what?" Jed said, his head tilted back with the beer.

Radcliff pointed out to the water.

But Jed could care less. Wasn't anything they hadn't seen before, and why Radcliff was making a bother about it didn't make much sense. "A boat. So what?"

"It just appeared out of nowhere!"

Jed laughed. "You're drunk! Probably been there all day, floating."

It surely hadn't been. Jed may have had a good buzz going, but he was hardly sloshed. "No! I swear it literally appeared like a mirage or something!"

Jed was amused by his friend's behavior. Instead of caring too much, he decided it would be better—and funnier—to mock him. "That's it, Radcliff, a *mirage*."

Setting his beer down, he stood, his eyes locked on that black boat. "I'm going to take a closer look."

Sounded good to Jed, maybe Radcliff would bring that stink away with him too. "You do that, you do that. I'm going to rest right here."

Radcliff looked over at Jed and saw that he was already leaning back and closing his eyes.

I know what I saw, and I intend to find out just what the fuck this is.

He got about five feet from the water and called out. "Hello? Anyone there?"

It was disturbing, to say the least, and the way it sat there was all wrong. It was shimmering like a reflection without substance, not material, a composite sketch of something trying to be real.

"I said who's there?" He waited for a response that never came. The boat just continued to hover there in the water, seemingly oblivious to his presence. "Well, that ain't very neighborly like."

Glancing back to the trailer, he saw Jed over there in his chair. From the looks of him, with his mouth sagging open, the beer had claimed him, taken him for a rest. Seeing no help in the matter, Radcliff swung his glance back on the boat.

"Well, I'm going to get to the bottom of this despite what he thinks!"

Kicking his shoes off, he took a step out into the water. Right away it felt strange to him. Instead of water lapping his ankles, it felt more like oil or some such greasy liquid. He thought maybe it had something to do with the boat and left it at that. Still assailed with that weird feeling, he was determined to find out just what the hell was going on here. It *did* just pop into existence, at least that's what he remembered seeing. But maybe it hadn't. Maybe it was sitting there and he just hadn't seen it before.

A couple of steps away from its hull, he reached a hand out and brushed the surface, immediately pulling away. "Damn, that's hot!"

The boat responded to this with its engine roaring to life, water bubbling around, and agitating waves to roll up the shore. Radcliff felt mortal danger here and he started backing up, but as he did just that, the boat spun around and took him by the feet with the propeller, dragging him screaming underwater into the mouth of the blades that chopped through his belly and sprayed him around in red, bleeding chunks.

A sound out near the lake woke Jed from his nap.

Wiping his eyes, he looked out there but didn't see anything to worry himself over. But then he remembered Radcliff walking out there, and he wasn't there anymore. He stood and got a closer look at the shore.

"Now where'd that idiot get to? Radcliff!"

As his focus came in sharper, he saw something lumpy lying on the shore. He chuckled in his throat. "Idiot is passed out drunk. Better get him before he washes out to sea and drowns himself."

Staggering off the porch, he took his time to get there, the drink making him wobbly and queasy. Eventually making his way over there without falling, he saw that Radcliff's legs were underwater, leaving his torso up on the beach.

"Get up you idiot before you wash out into the lake and drown your sorry ass!"

Impatient by a lack of reply, Jed kicked at his friend to wake him. When that wasn't getting the proper results he wished, he forced him over with a foot and saw that everything he had been hiding was ripped away, torn down to the spine, gutted, and emptied like a Halloween pumpkin. The smell of blood thick and hot in the air.

"What the fuck!"

Just then a black boat appeared to roll out of a misty wall on the lake, coming for Jed who looked on incredulously at what he was seeing. His emotions were a bag with a hole in it, and he couldn't quite plug it or understand what was happening here— what had happened to his best friend.

"What the hell—*hey*, what are you doing!? *Slow the fuck down!*" he shouted, preparing himself to run.

The horn of the boat rang in his ears like the explosion of a canon, screaming with demonic triumph as it leaped out of the water, hurtling like a boulder onto

Jed, who could do nothing but shriek and cower to the shadow lengthening over him before it smashed down on top of him like a hydraulic press, squishing him to a red, leaking pulp.

14

They had been waiting there for what seemed to be hours but couldn't be more than fifteen minutes. Still, in those waters a lifetime had passed, and still they weren't seeing any sign of the Messiah or his ebony boat from Hell.

Barney decided to fill the time with some banter, no matter how much he would have rather kept quiet. But to do that would have been unnerving. "Why did you decide to eliminate the cult on your own?"

To Father Thomas, that was an easy thing to answer, but painful to remember. "No one was willing to help."

Barney had a feeling that's what it was. As sad as that might have been to think about. "I know you said the Diocese wouldn't assist, but what about local law enforcement?"

"Did it ever occur to you that high-ranking officials were part of the Brotherhood of Darkness cult?"

It hadn't. But the more he thought about it, the more it became clear as to why there was a shortage of manpower years ago. It was all starting to click in place, the gears churning. "Yeah, I guess that would explain all the job vacancies a few years back. I still think what you did was right. Had I busted in there that night, I would have done the same thing."

Father Thomas smiled. It felt good to have this man on his side. Though he was a sinner to the Lord, the man had the heart of a Saint. And possibly, in time, he could earn redemption. "Thank you. That's reassuring. I guess we'll sort it all out on the other side."

Barney smirked. "That's deep—"

A resonation of anger thundered across the lake like the arrival of a great blizzard, coming from within only meters of the bow. Both men stood, eyes wide, mouths agape at the boat billowing into creation on a bed of whipping black, smoky tendrils. The sound of that hellish reverberation echoed out again as they felt its vibrations deep in their chest, ringing in their minds.

After that, it waited. A silence hung between the three.

"What does it want," Barney asked in a whisper, afraid of maybe riling it into an action they couldn't hope to stop.

"He's *challenging* us," Thomas calmly said, aware of the darkness closing around them.

Barney felt his blood boil. *"Then let's catch his ass and send him to Hell!"*

Slamming the throttle down, the boat shot forward.

Messiah Ward's craft swung its bow in the opposite direction and raced off in a smoky column ahead.

Keeping speed wasn't a problem, as it seemed no matter the engine that powered that demon craft, it was purposely staying pace with its pursuer. Their faces wet with the spray of the lake, their eyes dilated and determined, they prepared themselves for whatever devious design the Messiah had in store for them.

Barney felt the wind and smell of the death in his nostrils. He wanted to send that monster back into the black caves from where he emerged. He felt a renewed sense of purpose out here on this lake, something he hadn't felt in a long time. It was driving him to stop this foul beast, the butcher of the lake!

Thomas prayed silently as they pursued his brother in haste. In some painful way, he wished for this to end peacefully. But that was impossible, he knew, because his brother had so long ago forsaken the vows that he took in the defense of God and all of his creations. He had fallen, much like Lucifer into the dominion of a Dark God. Now, Thomas just hoped this plan of theirs would work. If not, it could spell disaster for the entire community, and beyond.

Messiah Ward's boat began to fade and flicker as black smoke thickened and particles of purple light swam inside this shifting cloud.

They watched on unsure of what was taking place, apprehensive with fear, and before they could come up with an answer, the black boat faded into an obscure fount of violet sparks that blew away in the wind and scattered over the surface.

"It's disappeared!" shouted Thomas, wary of what was next.

Barney knew something bad was happening here. This wasn't over. It was just the beginning. Something about this particular spot maybe. He didn't know. "He's lured us out into the middle of the lake. He has something planned. Stay alert!"

Like a mirage to a thirsty man in the desert, the black boat appeared in front of them in a rippling heat of smoky waves and banners, its razor-sharp bow pointed right at them, its satanic horn blowing its shrieking sounds.

Father Thomas felt his heart sink into his gut. "So, the time has come."

"Let's finish this!" Ripping out his Glock, Barney's face twisted in anger as his voice grew loud, louder than the horn's blaring. "Come on Messiah Ward!"

So, he did. Messiah Ward directed his black vessel right at them like a missile, coming toward them with a crackling of purple electricity webbing the frame and smoke rising from its surface.

Barney felt the hate well up inside as he took aim and started popping off rounds. He wasn't sure if they were so much as making a dent, but he didn't give a shit. It felt good to shoot at that damn thing. Felt damn good to release some of the tension that had been building since they fought those things down in the cellar.

Father Thomas tore his eyes away from the black craft and grabbed the oaken cross at his feet. Muttering a few quick prayers, he held it aloft over his head. "In the name of God, be gone!"

The face of the cross came alight with cosmic brilliance that exploded with a bright beam in the shape of the cross that crashed into the surging vessel. Both light and boat detonated in a holy blue shower of fire, throwing Barney and Thomas onto their backs with grunts.

Recovering their senses, they quickly rose to their feet, staring out over the lake.

Barney felt a rush of relief in the absence of that boat. "It's over … *It's over!*"

Thomas looked unsure but felt good at what he had witnessed. To see the light of God forced through the cross, it brought him a feeling of redemption.

Perhaps God had thanked him after all. "It appears it is—"

Suddenly, from behind the boat, the water rained over them as a black form leaped its way from the deep, arms outstretched, claws fanned out.

Messiah Ward locked his arms around his brother, his face a sloughing, waxy runoff of blood and tallow, brains oozing from the sockets in pinkish trails. "*Not so fast*," the Messiah said in a voice clogged with blood and meat.

Thomas fought at his captor, struggling with the arms that held onto him like a lover, embracing tighter, a rush of heat searing through his flesh and into his marrow. He looked down below and saw the cross sitting there, fingers of white smoke rising from it. A thought came to him that curled his lips with a grin. Lowering himself despite the grasp on his body, he grabbed the cross with one hand and held it flush to his chest.

"Lash us together, quickly!"

Barney saw where this was going, and there was no way he could have a hand in this. It wasn't right. "But …"

"There's no other way!" grunted Thomas. "Now!"

Barney cursed under his breath as he took some rope and wound it around the two multiple times to the protesting growls and hissings of Messiah Ward.

Wound tight in the fibers of the rope, Thomas winked at Barney. "I'll catch you on the other side!" And over his shoulder, he shouted to his fallen brother in a voice of acid. "And *you* are going back to hell!"

With that, the good Father Thomas hurled himself overboard and the two of them splashed headlong into the lake, sinking below the surface where they continued to battle and struggle until the ropes came loose and now the cross was pressed against Ward where a blinding explosion rocked the boat on a mushrooming plume of foam as a beam stabbed up from below the surface and shot up into the sky in a radiating blue column of light.

Barney fell hard to the deck and watched overhead as the sky brightened and a searing flash of energy forced him to cover his eyes. And as quick as that appeared, everything went silent.

All was silent.

Barney leaned over the gunwale. He could see his face in the blue water staring back at him. But nothing else.

"Father Thomas," he said, falling back into his seat, the feel of the boat listing in the waves not bringing the comfort he had wished.

EPILOGUE

That first night, after Barney recovered from it all, he had taken a week's leave from work and spent it at home, drinking heavily and sleeping deeply. But mostly drinking. Because sleeping was too much for him. Whenever he dozed off, he would see Father Thomas, not as he remembered the man to be. But as something more than he could handle. Thomas was no longer whole but was falling apart, the skin draining off his bones in slimy bands, his eyes pulped, leaking from the sockets, and blood spraying from his mouth. It got to where Barney didn't want to close his eyes anymore. He wanted to keep them open, always open. You just never knew what you were going to see when you closed them. And it wasn't just Thomas, but other things too.

The first time he closed his eyes for some rest, he saw those shadowy phantoms from the cellar, only there were a hundred of them coming out of the lake in a wave of groans, trails of kelp over their backs and shoulders, cloaks sagging on bony frames, eyes leaking black juice. Some had daggers in their hands, others hatchets. And sometimes Messiah Ward was there with them, leading them forward in a massive effort to sweep the town away beneath their barbaric lust for blood.

It was frightening, how real these illusions became. That's why he preferred to keep the bottle handy, and when that wasn't pushing the demons back enough for him, he had the coffee on hand. It was a rough first week, to say the least. Not only was he plagued by these terrifying manifestations, but he was hearing things too.

Sometimes in the middle of the night, he'd wake right up from the bed, hearing that goddamn motorboat just outside his window, prowling through the dark woods. He would hear screams, whispers, and the calling of evil sirens out in the lake. It was all too real.

It took a massive amount of effort on his part to fight these thoughts and push them away. But eventually they just sort of passed on, gone, flitting into obscurity. It gave his mind some release. Because before that, he was getting to the point where the gun was looking mighty good to eat. He thought about it a few times and even felt the cold barrel on his tongue. But he could never bring himself to do it.

Instead, he started reading passages from the Bible, remembering certain lines Thomas had told him. Most of all, he would focus on the priest, try and see the man that had given his life away so easily to purge the evil. It helped Barney; helped him push aside these horrifying intrusions. And after a while, he was liberated from these horrors. Left alone to collect the pieces that had blackened.

Weeks had passed since the incident on the lake. Most folks turned a blind eye to what they had seen out there, what they knew. All had returned to its normal routine. Fishermen were lining the shores and out in their boats, heading back to camp with full stringers.

It felt right, everything felt so right.

To most that was.

To Barney, there was a piece missing.

He was walking through the graveyard, along narrow headstones, into the misty valley of the dead. For the last few weeks, all he could see was Thomas, could hear his voice, his wisdom. But most of all, he could still see that last expression on his face before his selfless act took his life and that of his brother, Messiah Ward.

It's the only way!

Maybe it was, maybe it wasn't. To Barney's way of thinking, the man believed himself to be a sinner in God's eyes. So, redeeming his ways, Thomas figured the best way to do that would be to sacrifice himself in the name of God. Barney had been struggling to keep his faith since that day. And it all seemed so much like a dream. One that had taken place so quickly and ended just as fast. It was like a flash of memories that had trouble finding a spot in his mind to latch on to.

He walked along in the grass, coming to a flat slab with a cross on it, the name Father Thomas etched into its stone face.

Reaching into his pocket, he pulled out a rosary, feeling it in his hand. He could still see the way the man rubbed at the beads like maybe they were his only link to all that was good in his life. He knew the Father would want it, even in death. He placed rosary onto the grave marker.

"You forgot this," he said.

There was no other reason for him to be here, so,

he said a few things under his breath, made the sign of the cross along his breast, and turned around—

Standing out there near the church was a man. It only took a second for him to recognize the kind face and the black clothes, the clerical collar. He wasn't really there, of course, but some sort of final projection of his mind before he could close away this chapter in his life for good.

Father Thomas, in his ghostly form, smiled at Barney, showing him there was hope after all, as long as you believed.

Barney raised his hand and smiled. It did him good to see the man again, even if it was a mere figment of mist that soon dissipated.

Stay at peace, old friend. In time, we'll meet again.

The following pages include various images from the film.

Used by Permission.

THE RETRO MASS MARKET
COLLECTION

COLLECT THEM ALL!

- ☐ HELLRAISER: THE TOLL
- ☐ FRIGHT NIGHT
- ☐ RE-ANIMATOR
- ☐ HARDCORE
- ☐ WISHMASTER
- ☐ HELLRAISER: BLOODLINE
- ☐ TITAN FIND
- ☐ CREATURE
- ☐ VAMP
- ☐ SCARED TO DEATH
- ☐ OF UNKNOWN ORIGIN
- ☐ MANBORG
- ☐ ATTACK OF THE KILLER TOMATOES
- ☐ THE SPECIAL
- ☐ TAMARA
- ☐ FORBIDDEN ZONE
- ☐ COMMANDO NINJA
- ☐ LONG WEEKEND
- ☐ THE ODD JOB
- ☐ BLUE SUNSHINE
- ☐ THE BARN
- ☑ MOTORBOAT
- ☐ HOUSE SHARK
- ☐ HOUSE SQUATCH
- ☐ SHE KILLS
- ☐ SPLICE
- ☐ CUBE

ENCYCLOPOCALYPSE
PUBLICATIONS

9 781960 721495